EBB
OF THE
RIVER

Richard C. Mears

WYNDHAM BOOKS
NEW YORK

DECORATIONS BY FRED MARCELLINO

Designed by Eve Metz

Manufactured in the United States of America

1 2 3 4 5 6 7 8 9 10

Library of Congress Cataloging in Publication Data

Mears, Richard C., date.
  Ebb of the river.

  Bibliography: p.
  I. Title.
PZ4.M486Eb   [PS3563.E2]   813'.54   80-10658

ISBN 0-671-61032-5

Dedicated to my wife, Joan,
to my daughters, Lisa and Lara,
and to those characters who inspired *Ebb of the River*

*What greatness had not floated on the ebb of that river
into the mystery of an unknown earth.*

—*Joseph Conrad*

cool fresh wind blows in from the northeast, stirring the bay into a crescendo of whitecaps. Black and wood ducks scurry, wing tips to the waves, blending momentarily with the wild beauty of the reflecting sunlight as it dances amidst fleeting images. Rising suddenly as the bay gives way to a narrow stretch of land, the flocks hasten over the bluff and fly swiftly across the narrow mouth of the Patuxent River, soon to be shadowed by the primordial cliffs of Calvert. Amongst the multitude of tidal creeks, the stillest, least-touched haunts of the Chesapeake estuary, they quickly disappear.

It was here at this inlet that Captain John Smith first saw the proud Patuxent and Massawomek Indians fight for dominance over its fertile shores. Today these tribes no longer inhabit the river's alluvial banks, but the green and snowy herons still play sentinel in the tidal pools. And the jasmine and forsythia and japonica still burst forth to greet the spring, as they have for millennia. No longer does the blue smoke of galley fires rise from the berths of mighty schooners, but the portals of this great river still enchant its viewers and beckon like the powers of Circe.

The Patuxent River is a Maryland river. The longest and the widest and the deepest, it spans the length of Calvert and St. Marys counties and extends well into the Appalachian foothills. Reddish-orange cliffs, stratified with Cenozoic history, jut down to the river's edges and along its tidal shores. Where there are no elevations, the rich, verdant farmlands softly undulate out into the river. The cattle are indifferent, and on hot days stand knee deep in the shallows, as Mr. Poe, the town's patriarch, would say, "lookin' like old fish cranes, happy and not knowin' they ain't fish."

It was on such languid summer afternoons when the town of Solomons Island slumbered under its canopy of large willow trees that Mr. Poe and I would talk away hours into the Elysian summer nights. His stories were diverse and entertaining and rekindled a life replete with a love for people and things of the river. He enjoyed the summer months the most, but it was in the autumn that he described the Patuxent waters as most splendid.

The river is deep blue and "clear as a fisherman's eye," Poe would say. There are days when a person can see twenty to thirty feet deep. "There'd be shadows movin'. Ain't nobody most the time but 'Big Jim' crab, nasty and right cautious, mad the summer ain't no more.

"The river's not the same, son," he would say. "You don't see the darkies, do ya?"

He was right. When I was a lad I used to hear the blacks singing on the river almost every morning. Their oarlocks hummed. Their deep voices came off the water like echoes and rose sweet as flowered birds along the misty shore. Now only old, bent poles mark dead oyster beds. And the fish don't school anymore. Not even pogy.

Poe justifiably told me that I was not old enough to

know what the river was really like. He said, "The river's got a new breed" and "the fish hawk don't 'sociate no more." The narrow-hulled "bugeyes" and the hardy "skipjack" boats that once reigned over the mighty Chesapeake are scarce. Even the old sidewheelers, once the monarchs of charm and excitement on the river, are now archaic and long forgotten.

The towns along the Patuxent River have not changed much since 1862, especially the town of Solomons Island. It is a town of fewer than 450 people, nestled within the protection of natural breakwaters at the mouth of the Patuxent River. You would not recognize Solomons as an island unless you took time to notice. If you viewed the island from the air, you would say it resembled a briar pipe. A small white wooden bridge crosses over a tidal stream and connects the island with the rest of Calvert County. The town's kids like to brag that "jumpin' from Jay Bob's gasoline station to the island and back ain't nothin'."

Pale-yellow and teal-blue houses sit serenely on the river's edge. There are a few buildings that look strange and no friend to the sky, but the town's beauty prevails, festooned with honeysuckle and wild grapes and an abundance of sunshine.

When the river is quiet, the town reflects a rainbow of color on its surface until the sun climbs high and the colors fade off to a Solomon blue.

Solomons people guard their privacy zealously, and when asked the exact location of the island, they will curtly reply:

"You know where the Chesapeake is?

"You know where the Patuxent River is?

"That's where it is."

The boat captains say that the island hasn't been touched like other towns of the Tidewater because of its location; that is, far enough to be distant, but not so far that an hour-and-a-half drive won't cure small-town jitters. The city people, especially those from Washington, D.C., and Baltimore, come for weekends or summer vacations. Some have even been so enthralled with local color that they bought summer homes along the placid shores. Then there are the "foreigners," who are usually awed upon its discovery. However good their intentions to revitalize the island's surroundings, these visitors soon detect a pride born of heritage, people steadfast in their convictions and self-righteous in their predominantly Protestant ethic. Poe was always quick to challenge any disagreement.

"City folk are always coming here trying to change us. Goin' to make Solomons Island into a boom town, they'd say. Nobody pays 'em any heed. Why, we already had our boom, bigger'n any boom they'd bring us!"

History books attest to that. At least to the "boom" that took place between the years 1867 and 1890. The island was originally a part of the Eltonhead Manor and known as Bourne's Island—a sleepy little haven bought by Alexander Somervell, a well-to-do farmer and sea captain thereabout. He developed it into a prosperous tobacco plantation and, needing proper facilities for portage, he increased his dock capacity and renamed the island Somervell Island. But it wasn't until a Philadelphia man by the name of Captain Isaac Solomon arrived that the stories began to catch fire.

"Land sakes alive!" Poe related. "You woulda thought gold been struck! Big paddleboats came from all over, bringin' in people by the thousands! Isaac Solomon! Bigger and meaner than a hundred timber wolves. See all those shells piled mountains high? That's from Isaac an' his bunch. He turned this island into an oyster bed. First one in America!

"He was a smart one, that boy. He married a Somervell and got himself an island. Ha. Ha!

12

"Riverboats carried slaves in here by the hundreds. Them darkies shucked and cooked oysters till the town smelled like there weren't nothin' else. There was some carryin' on, I tell ya. There was gambling halls and smoking parlors. The only law was a yard spar and a ready fist.

"Why, even in the cold-weather months, when the wind came sweeping out of the nor'east, them people put on the biggest fish fries you'd ever want to see. Yes, sir! Them boys would get out there in the roughest weather and tong them oysters. Even the whites would work like blacks, dredgin' those oyster beds till their arm muscles ached and puffed out like blow toads. Sometimes it would come to shootin' and even killin' if someone got caught robbing the beds. There weren't no patrol in those days like now. It was quite a time, I tell ya.

"Come night, they'd come back to port to unload their catch and sit by a big hearth fire and smell them oysters fryin'. They'd drink their liquor. They knowed they'd got somethin'. The best thing was they knowed the next day was gonna be somethin' of the same."

The succeeding generations still live by the old notions of what constitutes right thinking, good behavior, proper upbringing, beautiful courtesy, and the simple pleasures.

"Good morning, ma'am!" "Crabbin' look good today, Ebb?" They always have time for a friendly and courteous "howdy."

The men are a lean and sunburned lot, honest as sounding rods, stubborn as mules and still the "reb." The women are a religious and proper sort and talk a good bit, especially about cooking. Hot breads, green-apple sauce, country-cured hams, and watermelon preserves. My mouth watered most of the time just listening. They always have their hair done up in the finest fashion and dress in colonial elegance. As with all

Tidewater people, they are a kissing, blushing, happy-go-lucky bunch.

Eli, the oldest black man in these parts, says "livin' in Solomons is easier than openin' you eye. All ya need is a couple of chickens, a hog, an' a good corn patch. Stalk yaself out a rabbit run; the river'll give you the rest!" It's not too hard to understand why Old Eli is a contented, happy man. "It didn't come easy," he admits. Eli descended from a slave family, as did most of the blacks in Solomons. You can't help but feel both elation and shame when you hear Eli sing his song:

> Ain't no boy own this river,
> Ain't no boy own this sky,
> Ain't no boy own this body,
> Goin' to Heaven when I die.

Although the river is a source of much life and goodness, it is also a river unrelenting in its journey, carrying within its awesome depths a treachery poised to destroy the unwary seaman.

The shore people respect the river with their deepest conviction, admonishing those who flout its power.

"Pay the river caution," they tell you. "Take too much for granted, you'll find out different. No one can outguess that river."

The river people have an uncanny awareness of nature's way, and as Ebb Kellum explains:

"Sometimes I can read near every notion she'll have. Other times, she don't tell nothin'. There are days she'll be slack and full o' the rainbow. I'd smell her perfume what come with the wind. And if I listen hard, I can hear the seasons whisperin' on. . . .

"But there will be times as bad when she'll raise off her bottom and slap you in the face. You don't believe she's the same river. One thing I know for sure," Ebb

14

exclaimed: "You gotta pay heed when she's mad, 'cus she don't care 'bout nothin' en nobody!"

Such was the event of one portentous day when William Bodecker and Ebb Kellum fished the mud slip at Half Pone Point. The river was slack and dead quiet. So quiet, according to Ebb, that voices carried great distances. Ebb realized the river was saying something. They looked to the oppressive sky. No birds flew.

"We's fools if we don't git!" Ebb warned. Bo looked to the sky again and shrugged his shoulders in resignation.

Looking across the river, the boys could see and easily hear a group of blacks in a boat. Ebb remembered them as having themselves a fine time. They were "liquored up and givin' no mind to anything." The hardhead were biting.

There were six blacks in the boat, and as Ebb explained, "the skiff set low in the water—too low for the size of the boat." A loud, ominous storm horn blew from the direction of Point Patience. Immediately, they saw two boats pull anchor and start in to shore. Instinctively, Ebb knew that he should have stopped fishing and hauled in the anchor. But Bo's fishing rod bent savagely down under the water. Bo said that he had hooked "the biggest fish in the whole world" and that he "wasn't goin' for nothin'." Just then Ebb's own pole jerked convulsively and bent completely beneath the hull, forcing Ebb to swing his rod around the stern. It was at that moment that they felt the first breeze—soft and willowy. Sinister. They had waited too long. Ebb hurriedly cut the fishlines as Bo quickly raised the anchor. However fast their reaction, a sinking, condemnable guilt prevailed as they desperately pulled together at the oars. In moments, they passed by the "happy" boat.

"God damn! Dat fish sure gonna pull you in. Ha,

15

haa . . ." Four of the blacks had "fish on." One large, fat man stood and threw chum aft and stared hypnotically as the mass of fish guts swirled over the water's surface.

Suddenly, dark, convulsive storm clouds heaved and rolled along the western horizon as if stalking their prey, and as quickly sped low and mercilessly over the river. In one great motion, the river rose with ominous force, and " 'fore we knowed it," Ebb said, "we stared at a wall of rainwater comin' fast as lightnin' across the west." A wave blotted out the sky and swept the fragile boat before its crest, speeding the skiff toward land and into shallow water. The skiff slammed into an oyster pole and turned astern. Waves boiled in, tossing the boat in their fury and pitching the dory high and over and toward the shore. Bo and Ebb, confused by this sudden chaos, struggled for shore. Hail came with the wind, pelting the river with unrelenting fury. Waves continued to sweep them forward until they touched shore and lay flat to the shifting sand. The storm subsided as quickly as it had begun. Bo and Ebb came up and out of the sand like two scared sand crabs, bedazzled and weary. Dark, fleeting clouds thundered off down the Chesapeake Bay, leaving the Patuxent River muddy and rough in their wake. They looked out over the water. "We knowed them niggers dead for sure."

CHAPTER 2

ESPITE its occasional disrepute, the river nurtures a substantial life anticipated and revered by all who share its seasons. In spring, the dogwood always blossoms big and white. All the boat scraping is religiously done, and the river folk meticulously mend their fish and crab nets and wait patiently for Big Jim. Some of the old-timers feign skepticism and vent their displeasure in passing time. "Big Jim ain't gonna come this year. Why, the dang nor'wester ain't stopped yet. Blowed everything out. Even the water could be drunk."

However pessimistic, such talk didn't stop Chase Kellum, whom everyone knew as Mr. Ebb or, simply, Ebb. He was Mr. Poe's favorite subject and—deep within his heart—a son. Mr. Poe described Ebb as a cocksure boy of Southern upbringing who had a knack for blarney and an old mind for reason. His core was surely enmeshed with nature, and he spent his waking days exploring its mysteries. Ebb knew the river and its inhabitants better than anyone else in Solomons. No one could recall a time when Ebb had come home empty-handed. He always caught his basket of fish and his bucket of crabs.

Ebb was duly baptized Chase Ezekiel Kellum. His Grandma Margie Kellum changed his name three times before she felt him worthy to be christened in the proper respect and seriousness of a church ceremony. As to his nickname "Ebb," that was indeed a tale Mr. Poe told with relish.

It was in the spring of 1946. Ebb had come of the age to be allowed to go skiffing alone. Such was the custom when a boy had proved himself in the art of watercraft, specifically if he could swim well and knew enough to protect himself from the sun. One summer morning Ebb had gone off in search of soft-shell crabs when he came to a place called Nelson's Cove.

This cove, like many of its kind in the Patuxent estuary, was the receptacle of large deposits of sediment brought in with the spring runoff. Such is the refuge for much of the sea life, especially for the molting crabs. The crabs' soft state leaves them prey to many carnivorous crustaceans and fish. The soft mud deposited by the river and the abundant algae that grow within its boundaries afford a protective covering for these wary crustaceans until their perilous transition from soft to hard has been consummated and they are able to maneuver in the wandering tidal currents. It is in this southeastern tributary that, on a full moon, the tide rises four feet and holds within its grasp the biggest soft-shell crabs to be found and caught thereabouts. Such was the intention of Ebb Kellum.

Gossip had it that the white folk stayed away from Nelson's Cove because it was near Shanty—the place where the black people lived. Ebb often heard tales about the white men found dead at Nelson's Cove. "Sure as you stand there, they'll kill you! Looka what those black bastards done to Prune! Doc Cobb said he drowned. But you know . . ."

It was a calm, sunny morning. Ebb stood on the bow

18

of his skiff and poled leisurely along the quiet, awakening shore, searching the potholes for soft crabs. The early mornings are the best times to catch these crabs, since the heat of the day has not boiled the water and the crabs remain undiscovered from the previous night.

Ebb said that he was "just passin' by" when he accidentally woke up a large soft-back turtle nestled in the mire. Startled, the green turtle rose up quickly from its hole. It swam vigorously and directly beneath Ebb's boat, leaving a trail of muddy water up to the shanty slough. Ebb, in his excitement, jumped to the stern and hurriedly poled to catch up to the frightened greenback. His momentum carried the boat smoothly and agilely across the water until, clumsily, he crashed into the old, broken hull of a partially submerged boat and was pitched headlong into the murky water. The boat careened sideways off the sunken vessel and floated away from Ebb. The river was low, and the shoreline had receded three feet, allowing Ebb to stand up and take hold of his bruised ego. He splashed water on his face and began to retrieve his boat. However, after the first step he sank deeply into mud up to his knees and there was held faster than a suck fly.

The barnacled hull of the sunken boat which stood big before him partially hid him from the shore. This made him thankful, for it was indeed a good hiding place from whatever reputed killers there be. And so he stood, not daring to holler for help for fear of waking them up.

The sun rose higher and the day became uncomfortably hot. Horseflies buzzed his head.

"They waitin' on my carcass. White worms gonna eat your heart; eat your eyes; eat you all," he thought.

As the tide continued to ebb, he watched his boat float slowly out toward Gimlet Pass. A big white crane flew lazily along the shore and landed in the shallows close to Ebb. He curiously watched the large bird stalk and with facility snap up minnows in his long elegant bill. As the mud cleared in the water around Ebb's legs, he spotted an old crusted blue-shell crab crawling in cautiously toward him. The crab, suddenly recognizing the unnatural obstruction, raised its claws defiantly at the intruder and slowly crawled backward and away to the deep channel.

Irritably, Ebb tried to move his feet again. Instead he sank further into the mud. No boats came in sight. He rubbed mud over his face and arms to cool and protect his skin from the relentless sun. Rolls of seaweed lay stranded on the drying shore and smelled of decay. Ebb, tired, leaned his head against the old hull and closed his eyes, when he heard the unmistakable sound of footsteps moving heavily across oyster shells. Ebb said that he "shrunk to my eyeballs" and peeked around his hiding place. An old, white-bearded black man wearing hip boots walked across the shady knoll. Ebb, bereaved by the occasion, quickly poked his head in back of the hull and froze stock-still, praying to God it was not his end. The footsteps stopped as suddenly as they had begun. It was in Ebb's anxiety and anticipation that he felt an intrusion like a "thousand flies." The silence became absolute and desolate, and seconds passed which seemed like eons to the frightened boy. Slowly, wearily, he looked around the broken hull. Again, and much to his surprise, he found himself staring directly at the old black man, who now sat on a wooden stump and, as Ebb remembered, "was smiling straight over to my left eye."

"Sure got you'self in a fix there, son."

"Yessuh!" Ebb said fearfully. He jerked his head in back of his hiding place and dared not show himself again. Convinced that this was "the end," he prayed what he knew from his Grandma Kellum's teachings

20

and held his breath. Fear swept through his body as beads of cold sweat formed on his forehead. Once again he started at the sound of footsteps and the splash of an oar as it tipped the water.

Before Ebb knew it, the black man looked down at him from atop his skiff and said, "Boy, you lucky stars is the ebb, son." He held out his big, brown arm, which glistened in the bright sun. "Hold on, boy!"

Ebb blindly obeyed and immediately latched onto the black man with both of his arms. The old man plucked him from the mire with ease and brought him into the boat, setting him gently to the deck, whereupon Ebb awkwardly stumbled to the middle seat. Thick brown mud oozed off his legs onto the deck. He was indeed surprised that his killing hadn't taken place and looked out of the corner of his eye at "that man smiling like an old fish cat."

"What's your name, son?" the black man asked kindly.

Ebb, vexed by indecision, said nothing.

"You tongue musta drifted out with the tide . . ." The old man thought for a moment. Suddenly, with a twinkle in his eye he said, "Suppose I call you *Ebb!*"

Ebb looked up at the man.

"What you say, Ebb?" He held his big, calloused hand out for Ebb to shake. Stubbornly, Ebb refused to move. But the old man persistently held his hand there until Ebb took it thankfully. Ebb remembered—"We both had smiles brighter than the sun."

CHAPTER 3

EBB'S reputation in Solomons Island was favorable by most standards. You could be sure that if there was mischief, Ebb was about. His ever-wandering, intense blue eyes and his wind-blown, reddish hair always gave him an air of curiosity and mischief, yet his image was subtle enough to get him by with whatever he had in mind. A puppy dog couldn't have been more effective. His wiry Irish frame bespoke Rockwell's portraits of young men, naive and captivatingly appealing in their manner, yet resourceful and determined in their endeavor. A handsome lad.

However impeccable his demeanor, Ebb's inner world dutifully avoided the confinement of a classroom. To wit, Ebb had an aversion to school. It wasn't that he didn't like going to school, it was that he liked *not* going to school better, and although Ebb spoke of it occasionally, Mr. Poe hesitated to describe Ebb's words as *kindly*.

"School House wasn't a big school, that is, if you looked at it from the outside," Ebb explained. "Nothing ever happened much. Old cock weather vane blew over in a northwest storm and stayed that way as long as I can remember. In the summer, School House would be newly painted and everything would be set trim. It even made me proud that it was 'my school.' But come the autumn, she looked like a red-white peanut butter 'n' onion sandwich; dried hard and crusted white—gonna swallow you up, Ebb.

"Sixth grade was the biggest class. It had six people and was taught by Sister Edwards. Actually, she taught all the grades at once, 'cept for the seventh and eighth grades. Sister was nice or mean, depending on who you were. 'Good-for-nothin's' is what she said was most of us—a breed of polecat what the devil only knows. Sometimes I thought she was right in her judgment, especially considering the carrying-on and all."

The events that began that sixth year were normal by Solomons standards. According to Ebb, it was the year they had "a thousand air-raid alerts and ten thousand fire drills." The air-raid alerts were the best, he recalled. They sat in the cloak room and sang patriotic songs and, as he described, "really saw each other." There was Colvin Corless with his cauliflower ears and Miss Marabel DePeu, a high dimpled young lassie with cherry red lips to whom he gave his saving stamp money. And Willie Veal Jones, a little black boy in the fifth grade. "Had a lice nest in his hair. Yes, sir! One day he come to school with a stocking on his head. He told everybody that he was a pirate—that he had special privileges. After that, all he did was show his 'dicky' to all the girls.

"Oh, yeah—and Jimmy Betts, who I didn't know too well. He got killed by his horse." Ebb's verbal reunions were always colorfully depicted and fondly recalled—sometimes sad.

Because he sat by an eastern window and could see the Patuxent River, the sixth grade had a special appeal to Ebb. He spent many pleasurable moments looking out over the long green shores and the white

23

beaches. It was a safe seat, as Ebb recalled, " 'cus of a mouse called Jeffers." Ebb insisted:

Jeffers was a social sort and would do most anything we wanted him to do. When Sister would come to scold, we would throw a piece of our lunch at his hole. Then he would come a-runnin' out of that hole like it had cats in it, stand his ground and nibble away at what we'd thrown. He'd eat anything just to scare Sister. No lie! She never came close when Jeffers was around. I can see her shaking her finger now. "You boys just wait!" she would scold. Well, the day soon came when we didn't have to "wait" anymore.

Sister was climbing a ladder to get paper out of her top closet. Near the top, she reached up high and stood on her tiptoes. It was right then that Tom Bon got the notion to pinch Mary Farquar under her seat. He done it in a fashion that weren't becomin' a gentleman, and Miss Mary jumped clean out of her desk screaming like you wouldn't a believed. Sure enough, Sister Edwards lost her balance and fell off the ladder, bouncing off the bottom rungs. She layed still to the floor. We thought she was dead. Some of the girls screamed and started to cry until they saw the Sister move her leg. When she finally came together, she sprang up off that floor madder'n a blow snake. Her eyes were blazing like fire and you could hear her wheezing as she sucked air. She was somethin' to see. She stood right where she fell shaking from head to foot. She didn't say a word. Then she limped over to Tom Bon.

Now, he was sitting there like an angel, with his hands folded nice on top of his desk. His eyes stared straight ahead. Jeffers sat where he was supposed to, eating the crumbs Tom throwed to him. You coulda sworn Tom had nothing to do with any of this. But he wasn't foolin' Sister. She near stepped on Jeffers when she grabbed Tom by his hair, fast and hard. She plucked him out of that seat like you would pick a carrot. His long legs came out from under the desk, half kneeling, half standing. He said he was sorry a million times. But it weren't no good. When she hit him, his head went bobbing like a loose buoy. Next day, Tom Bon told us, " . . . she's a dirty nigger, German, Jew bastard"—and that he was gonna kill 'er for sure. But he never did.

Although the sixth grade had been exciting for Ebb, it was the Strawberry Festival that he anticipated most. This event marked the beginning of the summer and the end of the school year. All the school kids and townspeople dressed in their Sunday best for the "School House Show." Even old Mr. Poe, Ebb described, "wore the best he had for such an occasion, a black suit and a real bow tie with shoes a-shinin'. He was the most anybody ever seen." Indeed Poe was distinguishable. Pure white hair bedecked a deeply tanned face, wrinkled and aflow with wisdom and life's happiness. His nose was large and uneven. His teeth were proudly referred to as *his*. They were yellow from tobacco stain. His small eyes twinkled. Bandy-legged he was but still quick moving at ninety-two. His large, leathery hands and stubby fingers were strange to his small frame and bespoke hard work and honest time.

The festivities began when Miss Carol and Miss Young sang "God Bless America." The audience stood. Ebb thought the singing was awful, but as he recalls, most of the people liked what they heard and clapped enthusiastically. Once everybody was seated, Mrs.

25

Eastwood, the mistress of ceremonies, waddled to the middle of the platform. Ebb thought she was the ugliest, fattest teacher in the school, but assured me that she was also the nicest. "Even though she wasn't a 'Sister,' " he said, "she always treated ya like you was the best thing she knowed."

Mrs. Eastwood made a general announcement and then introduced the first event. "Miss Sara Newborn, ladies and gentlemen!"

Marching music blared out from two large loudspeakers that hung high and in front of the stage. Miss Newborn strutted out twirling a baton and stepping smartly. Her pants were tight and Ebb remembered her cheeks bouncing up and down—"whack-i-dy-slack."

The Reverend Thornton sat relaxed and smiling, his big jowls spread out like he was the happiest thing alive. Ebb knew it to be only pretense. Perspiration dripped off the Reverend's face.

For the moment, this wasn't the happiest time for Ebb either. The events that followed caused Ebb much anxiety. Sister Edwards had persuaded Ebb to recite *his poem* at the Strawberry Festival. He was next to perform, and as Ebb recalled:

"Just like that, I got scared. More scared than I ever been." Ebb had never seen so many people in one place. He held tightly to his chair and looked down at his new white shoes. They were big and puffy and made his feet hurt. He repeated the first line of his poem over and over again to refresh his memory. But as the occasion would have it, two of his friends, Fasso, known as "Jelly Belly," and Top, a true half-Powhatan Indian, sat mischievously beneath an old oak tree, laughing and spreading their mouths in all kinds of contortions for Ebb to see. Ebb tried not to see their frolicsome ways, but the more he tried, the more they drew his attention. It was because of curiosity and his own ras-

26

cally ways that the inevitable happened. He indulged their vicarious pleasure until the sudden realization and terror of stage fright absorbed his mind. "I thought I'd go blind," he remembered. "My seeing got blurred. I shook my head and came to focus on a pair of hands, nice hands, that seemed to move like spiders. They moved across a purple ground. Looking up, slow, blue eyes were there, strong and prying." It was Mrs. Dabb, sitting up front. Behind her, Ebb saw Runk, the chicken farmer. Ebb's mind wandered.

"Yella and green teeth he had, and smell like a pig. The chicken, neck in hand, and Runk's knife a-swingin'. Bloody he make 'em. Into the barrel. Thump, thump. They died so slow."

Ebb frantically shook his head again. But the visions came on even stronger: of Black Tate—a Swahili tongue and a black cat. The cat screamed, its shrieks fading to a death gargle and silence. The sensation spread through Ebb's body like a mystic fog. He sat in his seat in awe until he heard a faint whisper in the quietness:

"Ebb. Ebb Kellum . . ." Ebb heard the name repeated again and again. The voice became louder until the vision passed. Looking up, Ebb saw Mrs. Eastwood staring down at him in bewilderment. "Get up there!" she whispered. "You're reciting next."

Ebb felt sick in his stomach and wanted to run. But there was no way out of his reciting, except dying, he thought. Top told Ebb after the occasion that "you bones jumped out the seat," and that he had stood silent for a long time. Suddenly, Ebb had shouted out loud, "A tongue lashed out . . ."

Top said that he stopped and started—"you was like a locomotive once you got goin' . . . the poem come out like a whistle." The audience was stunned. As Ebb finished he sat down quickly. He didn't know whether the audience was "clapping or shooting." Mr. Poe stood up and applauded. He shook his head approvingly to all about him. Mrs. Eastwood was as "proud as a buttercup." She walked over to Ebb and got him to stand again. "I didn't want to," he said. "I thought for sure that she was gonna make me tell the poem again." But she didn't. Instead, she said out loud, "He wrote it himself!"

Everybody applauded again—this time with more enthusiasm.

The next day, Grandma Kellum showed Ebb the *Prince Frederick Herald.*

" 'The Rivers' by Chase E. Kellum."

Ebb gave it little thought until Top took a paper clipping from his pocket and showed it to him.

"Ain't that you?" Top said. "My ma says it is."

With much aplomb, Ebb assured him that it was. Top held up the piece of paper for Fasso to see, only to have Fasso snatch it from his hand. He read the clipping disapprovingly.

"How'd you know 'bout the . . . 'bout . . ." Fasso searched the poem and pointed to one of the rivers' names—"Cho . . . Cho-pa . . ."

"Choptank," Ebb said authoritatively. He pointed to the names of all the rivers and recited the poem again.

When he finished, Top put his hand to his head, pretending disbelief and looked to Fasso for a similar response. "Ain't that Ebb," he said joyfully.

Fasso irritably gave the news clipping back to Top. "Anybody can recite if they want to. Writin' ain't so hard!" But Top firmly stood his ground and said that there wasn't a person who could do better. It was Ebb's proudest time.

CHAPTER 4

She heard the angels calling
From off the Heavenly shore
So she flopped her wings
And flew away
To make one angel more.

Martha Johnson
Born February 1897–Died March 1947

O one remembered Ebb ever to have cried before. He tried to stop the tears, but there was no stopping what he felt. Martha Johnson had been the "mammy" of the Kellum family since Ebb could remember. She was a big woman, as Ebb recalled. "The biggest I ever seen. Soft and warm. She'd hold me tight to all her bosom and sing her song and I'd go floatin' off."

She called Ebb "son" until the day his Grandma Kellum heard her. She reproached Martha for her "assumptions" and told her to never do it again.

Ebb's most feared premonition happened all too suddenly. Martha always went out visiting at night. "Now Ebb," she would say, "you behave youself while old Martha takes a visit. I be back soon." She would lean over and look straight into Ebb's eyes. ". . . I don't, the good Lord'll be borrowin' me." She would hug him "with all the love there is"—and go her way.

Then, one day she didn't come back. All Ebb remembered seeing was her bigness in the ground and everybody sorry. Black folk came from great distances to pay their respects. Their homage surprised Ebb since he knew only of her daily routine around the Kellum household and of her sleeping quarters in the large pantry by the kitchen. He figured there must have been at least a hundred people around singing and praying. Even his Grandma and Uncle Kellum came to the funeral and stood amongst the blacks praying silently. Just before the service was over, "Hot Dog" Lincoln solemnly placed a plate of food and two bright, porcelain yellow cups on the grave. Ebb knew, however, that Martha wasn't one for drinking from a cup. So the next day, Ebb found her favorite "bottle" in the pantry and laid it by her side.

Ebb had lived most of his life with his Grandma and Uncle Kellum on top of Periwinkle Hill. The "Kellum Mansion," they called it. It was a large house of eleven rooms, built in 1878. Its construction was Queen Anne style, or what they called in those days "free classic" —a generous adornment of gables and latticework. French-gray clapboard interspersed with ornamental shingles and roofed with red slate made it quite stunning. The trimming was painted a salmon-pink tipped with Indian-red chamfers. And then there was the large fireplace in the living room made of black bricks where logs burned and crackled all through the winter and into the spring, giving warmth to all the family. In the summer the family would sit out on the screened porch or under the large oak tree where the view stretched out over the Patuxent River for three miles to the southeast.

30

Ebb didn't have too many complaints about his chores at the Kellum home except for toting water from the old artesian well. That was mainly because he had to do most of the toting. The well had to be drilled a good distance from the outhouse. And of course, under Grandma Kellum's supervision, this meant it was on the opposite side of the main house and twenty-five yards beyond. The well was friendly yet formidable, old with moss and a patina of time. In its darkness he could only see the water level when occasional light scanned its surface. At times, Ebb would close his eyes and slowly let the water bucket down into the well. "Accidentally" he would loose his grip just for the pleasure of hearing the bucket slap the water and bubble out of sight. He said it was worth the wait for a "clean bucket," using the word "clean" loosely, mind you. Few people knew, as Ebb explained, what concoctions graced the artesian depths. Aside from the iron content of the water, he did admit reluctantly to another exotic ingredient.

One day, Top and Ebb found a big, bushy raccoon caught in one of their muskrat traps. The steel jaws of the trap held the 'coon tightly, and, as Ebb explained, "near chewed his leg off. The 'coon wasn't about to let us take the trap off 'em." Blood matted the fur of his hind leg. This annoyed Top, and with sympathetic resolve he persuaded Ebb that they should wash him thoroughly. In due course, the raccoon ended upside down on the long thin end of a bamboo pole, and off to the well they went.

Once at the well, they held the 'coon aloft, over the well, while attempting to tie the bucket rope to the trap chain. Suddenly, the raccoon lunged at Top. More surprised than scared, Top screamed and let go of the trap, 'coon and all. Margie Kellum on hearing the commotion excitedly flew out the door, ran down the

kitchen stairs, stopped long enough to survey the "ca-
lamity" and then walked hurriedly past the boys and to
the well.

Confused at first, her eyesight slightly impaired with
age, she momentarily looked up out of the darkness
and blinked her eyes. She looked down the well again,
and once assured of her impression, she said earnestly,
"Ebb, your uncle is going to thrash you. Get that animal
out of this well!"

"I didn't drop 'em!" Ebb said defensively. He looked
at Top for verification.

Top had hardly opened his mouth before Margie Kellum had pointed a firm finger down the well and emphatically repeated, "Ebb, you get him out of this well
right this minute."

Ebb and Top looked down the well. The raccoon was
struggling desperately to stay on the surface. But no
sooner would it get a breath of air than the heavy trap
would pull the raccoon under the water again. The
'coon surfaced eight times before losing its energy and
succumbing to death. Ebb said that he "ain't felt
sicker."

His Uncle Elton didn't take too much of a notion to a
dead raccoon being submerged in the drinking well and
directed the boys to fetch him out of the water as fast
as they could—"even if you can't." After an hour of
concentrated supervision, Ebb finally hooked the now
heavy carcass and pulled the ill-fated raccoon to the
surface and out of the well with his trot line. As he
remembers, "I weren't gonna drink water from that
well no more. But Grandma made me tote water from
Jess Robinson's place next door—quarter mile away.
After two weeks, they finally said the well was safe
enough for drinking. They gave me the first drinking
privilege, and so I did. Between you and me, it tasted
like raccoon guts, hair, and eyeballs, but I weren't for

telling 'em. They drank the water and said it was pure, cold and delicious again. I thought sure they'd die."

Margie Kellum brought Ebb up as a Methodist although she sent him to a parochial school. She said it was "the best school for these parts," but only for the 3 R's. Other than that, she was Ebb's tutor by the strictest Methodist standards. She specialized in prayer, the polishing and teaching of which Ebb would never forget.

"Say the 'Our Father,' " she'd tell Ebb, and he would recite it. Inevitably she would say "it's wrong," "the school way," and commence to repeat the prayer the right way, "as the Methodists are taught."

Ebb fondly remembers his Grandma Kellum as a saintly woman. Good, but blinded by tradition. Steadfast in her thoughts. A rock. She was a true matriarch. And he loved her deeply. He always heard stories from the townspeople about what a fine-looking woman Margie Kellum had been, and all the "suitors" she had call at her door. Ebb never believed the gossip because she wasn't exactly what he called "pretty."

Although Ebb had the deepest respect for his Grandma, her incongruity in task and sentiment toward black people annoyed him. She was unreasonably "hard" in her relationships with blacks and totally apathetic to their needs. Ebb recalled:

My Grandma got sick during the birth of my Uncle Ezra. My Uncle Elton told me that the doctor thought she'd die. Ezra was a big baby. Twelve pounds. One of the black mammies who had given birth at near the same time nursed Ezra until he got bigger. But you know even after that, Grandma never let that black mammy sit down with us to eat at the big table, not even at Christmas. Heck, my dog Honker always came like he pleased and sat by my chair for scraps—which was considerable at times.

Even when people visited, she would make them keep their Negroes in the shed house. But the darkies liked that. One day I sneaked up to hear 'em carrying on.

"You pussy-eating man. Ain't you ever gonna find a woman who stand up and look you straight to the eye?"

They all got to laughin' and horsin' around.

"Why is you a mother-fucker, Roe?"

Roe said back, "Only mother I ever fuck's yours."

They got to fighting and got powerful mad. I never seen any cutting. But there was a big ruckus and all the white folk came out. They thought for sure the big buck, Roe, was dead. But he was only knocked out and got a big lip.

"They never take a bath," Top told me once. "Honest ta God!" he said seriously. "You smell 'em? Dey smell like bacon, fish and urine, all the same time."

I didn't believe that either, nor thought about it much. But the next time I got near a nigger, I got to smelling more than usual. They really ain't smelled like all he said and even different so that you couldn't tell who's gonna smell like what. Then one day I got to thinking about Grandma and how she said never once did she let a nigger touch her in her whole life. And when I thought harder, I didn't recall having touched one either. The nearest I got was in picking up Willie Jones's coat. He always lost his coat in the school yard. One day I picked it up on the end of a stick and gave it to 'em. Sister Julia seen me and said that I should be ashamed and made me hold the coat in my hand

and give it to him. I held the coat with two fingers, but that wasn't good enough for Sister. She made me hold that coat with my whole hand.

Anyway, Martha had touched me a million times. I knowed that. But I ain't really touched her just for touching. I fixed to touch her. It was on a Saturday morning. Martha stood over the stove, browning potatoes and fish fillets for the family.

"Mornin', Ebb!"

"Good mornin'!" I said casual. I walked over to the ice box and pretended to be looking for something.

"You gettin' hungry, child?" she asked. She flipped the potatoes over. They sizzled and sputtered and made puffs of potato smoke. I stood there wondering where I was gonna touch her, because it was my intention to touch her right on the skin.

"What you need, Ebb?"

I shook my head and watched the fish frying. She was getting uneasy, I suspected. I used to sneak up behind her in much the same way when I was smaller and give her fanny a good swat with a stick occasionally. Strangely enough, feeling came over me. I felt naked and my pecker-head stuck straight out. I all but turned away in embarrassment when she turned around and pretended that she was going to hit me with the spatula.

"Land-a-sakes, child! What is wrong with you? You get ready for breakfast like the other folks is doin'."

I grabbed her scoldin' arm. It took just a second and I ran out of the kitchen as fast as I could.

"I don't know what's gettin' into you, child. Ummmmm-mmmmmm," she mused, and went back to cooking.

My hand smarted like Top said it would. I smelled it and ran out to the bucket and washed it good. It stopped hurting. That was really somethin'!

CHAPTER 5

EVERY Monday night, the Kellum dinner table was set in abundance. Colorful as a county fair, spread full of leftover food from the past week and enriched with sturdy earthenware. Each plate was bright, buttercup yellow, embellished with a Rhode Island rooster—Ebb's favorite dinner set. It was on such a Monday that Ebb's Aunt Hattie and Uncle John drove down from Prince Frederick for an evening visit. For the occasion, Margie Kellum steamed whole blue-shell crabs in beer and Old Bay seasoning. The big kettle top seemed to jump with glee as steam escaped into the kitchen air, filling the house with an aroma befitting a Bacchic feast.

It was custom to set out the hot spiced, crimson-red crabs on long wooden tables whereupon they cracked their shells with large wooden mallets and picked out their sweet meats. The broken shells were stacked high in the middle of the table. Later, they would be deposited in the vegetable garden. That night, however, the dinner was served in polite formality to celebrate Uncle John's sixty-fourth birthday. Simply, according to Ebb, they were to eat as gentlemen and ladies. Margie Kellum even set out her crystal finger bowls for the auspicious occasion.

Ebb admitted that cracking hard crab shells like a gentleman was not easy. He watched intently as his Uncle John expertly attacked the meal. With elbows raised unusually high, his Uncle John leaned vampirishly over the heavy table. With forearms bent slightly forward and fingers poised, carefully touching this crab and that crab, he selected a large one with his big, calloused hands. Holding it aloft, he fastidiously broke off each claw and with sudden felicity snapped the protective shell, exposing its meats. It was a buster. He broke the body in half and commenced to separate each fat appendage, tearing each one in quick order and setting the white pieces of crab meat carefully on a plate, unmindful of how the succulent morsels tantalized the eyes of those watching. Dutifully, he gave one plate to Margie Kellum, another to Aunt Hattie and then asked Ebb if he would like the same done for him. Confidently, Ebb answered a polite "no." In like fashion to Uncle John, Ebb held his arms high and selected a good-sized crab. Having established his individuality, Ebb began to pull industriously at the big, red shell. As Ebb explained, "The whole crab came apart faster than a hen's leg." Juices squirted out in all directions and dribbled conspicuously down his white, linen shirt.

"God damn!" he shouted.

Ebb's words froze everyone in motion. Eight eyes stared incredulously in his direction—and Margie Kellum cried out, "God have mercy!" Hastily and with unmitigated desperation, she rose from her chair and collapsed on the porch couch. There, she murmured several supplications pleading the Lord's forgiveness.

Finally, Uncle Elton put the occasion at ease. With stern presence and forthright determination, he addressed Ebb. "Young man, would you mind repeating what you just now said?"

Ebb, amazed at his own linguistic agility, took satisfaction, however treacherous to his upbringing. It was at this moment that he first experienced the intuitive awareness of a third influence—the subtleties of the subconscious—imposed on what he had originally considered insignificant. Judging from the dire expression on Margie Kellum's face, Ebb knew he dared not repeat himself nor tell where he had heard the loathsome expression. It was indeed a moment of courage and dedication, Ebb explained. "I wasn't gonna be a traitor to Fasso, the best cusser in the world—and the best teacher of the same." Then too, Ebb rationalized, it was at such a cussing session that he came to meet William Bodecker. As he remembered back on that auspicious moment, he took his whipping courageously.

The aforementioned incident had happened on the first day of August. This was the day that Ebb consciously thought of, and said, his first curse word, "God damn!" He had indeed heard words equally as profane, which the donor had rendered with indisputable relish. But the words "God damn"—that was indeed the ultimate whammy!

It had been a hot, clammy day. Ebb and Fasso were sitting lazily under Ebb's big oak tree, sipping lemonade and looking sheepishly out over the sultry, calm Patuxent River, when Top ran up, huffing and puffing. He stood glassy-eyed and held his side from pain. He waited until he caught his breath, and then, with urgent quickness, swallowed deeply and said, "They down at the fishin' hole."

With that, he collapsed to the ground and rolled over on his stomach. Bemused, Ebb and Fasso stared at Top for several seconds before Top turned toward them and propped himself up on his elbow. Looking straight into

Fasso's eyes Top solemnly said, "It's you hole, Fasso."
Ebb related the story:

Right then we knew a storm was comin'—
maybe a killing. There's nothin' worse than to tell
the whereabouts of somebody's fishin' hole, especially about Old Gray Hill where I know is the
best. It had taken Fasso a whole summer to find
that hole. That's no lie. I knowed where it was 'cus
Fasso let me fish aft. I vouched then in front of
Fasso, just like he done for mine, that if anybody
told where the holes was, that body would get
killed or whatever was worse.

"You sure it's my fishin' hole?" Fasso asked
unbelievingly.

"It's you hole, Fasso. I seen Pfeiffer and a nigger rowin' out with fishin' poles—and sure 'nough
— they's fishin'!"

"A nigger! What nigger?" Fasso shouted. "God
damn!" He was getting madder than a egg-layin'
rooster.

"I ain't seen 'em before," Top insisted.

Fasso grabbed the oak tree with both his arms
and squeezed it hard. He kicked it near ten times.

"God damn black whore!" he shouted. He
clenched his fist and went steamin' off toward
Miller's Bluff as fast as he could. We set out
walkin' with 'em and feelin' sorry for 'em. I got to
thinkin' that maybe the nigger might get a notion
to fish aft. That got me to thinkin' madder.

"God damn German, nigger, Jew bitches!"
Fasso yelled. Top and me repeated the same, only
we was whisperin' 'cus we didn't know such words
right then.

". . . black mother fuck . . . God damn . . .
bastard!" He said it a million times and even

louder. This made us walk faster, until we almost ran.

"Cock knockin', son-of-a- . . . dirty . . . flinchin' . . . BITCH!" he yelled.

We was runnin'!

The cussin' and name callin' came faster than we could think until all three of us hollered at the top of our lungs and raced like madmen for the ridge overlooking Miller's Point. At the top, sure enough, we saw Pfeiffer and the nigger out at the hole—fishin'!

Come four o'clock, we saw 'em headin' for Tuma's Pier. We were waitin' and ready. Fasso said that they oughta be hanged from Old Gray Hill. But Top and me said that was bein' too kind and would put a curse on the fishin' hole—that we had to stick to the pact and do what's worst. And we figured, what's worse than eatin' dog-do. Soon as we got down to Tuma's Pier, Fasso found a spot on the pier, cleaned it off with his foot and told us to find some "dog shit." Now I didn't ever see anybody eat dog-do, mind ya, so it seemed excitin' at the time. We got to lookin' and near couldn't find any until I remembered where Chester, an old bulldog, went. We ran down near the old oyster dock and sure enough, there was a good pile. We carried it on an old pine board. It was dried hard from the sun and didn't smell none. Fasso carefully set it in a neat circle. When we finished, we stood and looked curiously at it.

"Are we gonna make 'em eat it for sure?" Top asked.

"They fishin' in the fishin' hole, ain't they?" Fasso answered.

"But we don't know the nigger," I said.

"Sooooo . . . he's a nigger, ain't he? He ought

41

to eat it first." Fasso leaned over the pile and pretended he got the darkie by the neck. "I'm gonna push his face right in iiii . . . it till he knows whose fishin' hole it is."

"How's he know it's our fishin' hole?" I asked.

"He knows! Did you ever see anybody else there fishin' exceptin' us?"

"Pfeiffer showed 'em," Top said.

"Don't make no matter. A nigger's a nigger— and he gonna know it!" Fasso stood lookin' out to where the boat was slowly comin' up to the pier. A dragonfly landed on the long, white crusted mound —but didn't stay long and flied off in no certain direction.

The rowboat glided slow in the smooth water. Pfeiffer brought it 'bout with a stroke of his oar and then let his oars lay on the boat gunwale. The wharf shook when the boat hit and some of the dog pile rolled, but not much. Pfeiffer looked up. His long, drawn, skinny features made him look like he's going to sleep all the time. He grabbed on to the first pilin' to steady the boat, and moved slowly from pilin' to pilin' till he came to where he kept 'er tied. Crabs was swimmin' in the bottom of the boat where the seep water settled. Bo didn't look up. He pretended he didn't know we was there and right off started to clean the boat with an old fish rag.

"What ya catch?" Fasso said without letting on he was mad.

Perch, spot and a big hardhead layed in the bow. A toadfish was all cut up and spread out on the stern board. Bo looked like a river nigger for sure: strong and healthy, his skin shinin' slick and golden brown. He had brightness in his face and moved quick and right. He teased a crab with his toe. I thought that mighty good for a darkie.

42

Pfeiffer didn't say nothin', which is his way, and pointed to the fish. He held up the hardhead and we all looked at it close. It was the biggest I ever seen.

"Bodecker caught it," Pfeiffer said slow and looked at Bo. Bo weren't lettin' on he was proud; 'specially in front of whites. He continued to play with the crab. I was kinda glad the nigger caught it.

"What ya catch the hardhead on?" Top asked Pfeiffer.

"Peeler."

"He musta really pulled." Top took hold of the fish and made on like it weighed a ton. Fasso moved closer for a look and scratched his head.

"What time did you catch it?"

Pfeiffer shrugged his shoulders and looked down at Bo. Bo shyly turned his head to look up, when suddenly he bounced into the air and about sunk the boat. It scared us somethin' fierce. We all jumped back. A blue-shell crab went flyin' through the air and came down in the river. Bo sat in the bottom of the boat holdin' his toe like it was gonna fall off. He let out a scream like I never heard a nigger before. I thought sure he was gonna say "mother-fucker" and all that, but he didn't. He grinded his teeth and held to the boat tight. Then he half smiled and said, "Man, he bite!"

Not that we wanted to, but we got to laughin' until the pier near fell down. Pfeiffer couldn't help but laugh too. And that's somethin'. He done it snortin' on one end and buglin' on the other.

That was all right, for sure, till Pfeiffer and Bo got to totin' the fish and things toward home. Bo hobbled down the pier like a one-legged pirate. He turned around just before he stepped off the pier and said, ". . . ummmmmm, umm! Crab sure bites. OUUUUUeeeeee!"

Pfeiffer and his big feet near stepped on the dog mess. He looked down and seen it just in time and near jumped like it gonna bite. He gave it a big kick and sent the dog-do crumblin' all over the river. He shook his head and walked off, but didn't go far before he stumbled on a loose board. Top looked at me. I looked at Fasso. We near laughed ourselves to death.

CHAPTER 6

TO Ebb, the fishing-hole incident enhanced both an awareness of Bo and a curiosity as to the colloquialism often heard among some of the dock hands, "A nigger ain't real people."

Only two weeks had lapsed when Ebb saw William Bodecker again. Ebb, Fasso and Top always spent Saturday nights in town. They would go to the movies, and afterward play the pinball machines if they had made enough money from selling their weekly catch of crabs and fish. This particular night Ebb was with his elders. His Uncle Elton wanted a Sunday paper, and his Grandma Kellum had decided on a fresh chicken for the Sunday pot. In turn they volunteered to take Ebb and the boys for a sporting ride into town in the old yet mechanically sound Model T Ford. As they drove onto Mr. Jim McMannis' farm to pick up Top, Ebb noticed an old flatbed truck loaded with newly harvested watermelon. Bo was topside and about to jump down from the truck when he spotted the car and, on seeing Ebb, stopped short and stood curiously watching their arrival. It was on spotting Bo that Ebb leaned out of the window and enthusiastically waved to him. Bo shyly smiled and started to wave back, but instead hesitated

45

and shook his head in silent friendship. However casual the intent, the unexpected happened.

"Bull" Fury, the McMannis farm supervisor, rushed angrily over to the truck and pulled Bo off the truck with one quick motion.

"What the hell did I hire you for, boy! Just to stand around?" He grabbed Bo by his cheeks and shook his face indignantly. "Answer me!" Fury yelled. He cuffed Bo's ears.

Bo wiped his eyes with his forearm and said in a faint whisper, "Yessuh."

The foreman studied Bo's reaction and, once satisfied, took hold of Bo's neck and pushed him pitilessly toward the truck.

"You're not worth a God damn, boy! You know that? You tell your brother, if he wants work on this farm, he'd better get his hide here and not send me the likes a you. I've got enough to do . . . wet-nurse your kind." Fury turned and walked over to the Kellum car.

"Good evening Mr. Kellum, Mrs. Kellum," he said politely. He smiled infectiously at Ebb, and without addressing anyone in particular, said, "Sorry about the disturbance. Seems the only way to get this kind to work."

Margie Kellum had chosen not to watch the scene and had turned her face piously and unreproachably in the direction of the McMannis house. But now, confronted by Mr. Fury, she agreed wholeheartedly with his observation.

Fury had a fearsome reputation. The black people hated him and stayed away from the McMannis farm if they could. But there were times when they needed money and were forced to help him with his crop. Jim McMannis paid well and hired any able body, even white trash such as the one they called Fury.

Bo hung his head in embarrassment. Ebb was repulsed and felt a surge of emptiness. Sadly, Ebb slid back in his seat, into the shadows of the car. He had often thought it peculiar that neither Top nor Fasso nor himself had any black friends. Not that being black made any difference to him. A friend is a friend. He had liked Bo from the first time he saw him at Tuma's Pier and had made up his mind to befriend him. That is, until the day he found out that Bo was Jonas' younger brother.

As Ebb explained, "Jonas used to be a nice nigger." He would come to the Kellum house and work at various chores. When he saw Ebb, he would say kiddingly, "There goes that good-lookin' boy, Ebb. When ya gonna tell yo' secrets, Ebb? How ya parts growin'?"

Ebb said he never paid Jonas any attention, nor considered tainting his intentions since Jonas was the biggest black man that he knew in Calvert County—big for 20 years that is. He was also a "pretty nigger," with sharp, aquiline features resembling the Egyptians he had once seen in a history book. Even Jonas' hair was different from the hair of other blacks Ebb knew. It was set in shiny, black wavelets, always, as Jonas mentioned, being combed "for the women." Ebb often referred to his cousin Rachael's statement: "If more of our men looked like that black man, we wouldn't be just sittin', that's certain."

Ebb admired Jonas for his direct, independent nature. What most white people took as brashness and disrespect afforded Ebb a corresponding quality by which he came to judge and entrust his own camaraderie. However, Jonas, as he grew in Ebb's eyes, imposed a fear, a distinct and ominous threat. Though intrigued, Ebb kept his distance from what Fasso would call "peculiar and nigger" and would have remained distant had not an ironic twist of fate led Ebb mistakenly to wander into Shanty, helpless and confused, and thereby compound his apprehension.

Ebb's dog, Honker, had discovered a raccoon in the

woodpile one afternoon and chased it into the tidewater marsh. Ebb followed excitedly, listening to the baying hound as he headed south along the eastern shore flat and across the back wood into Russ's corn field and on toward the pine thicket. After crossing the flat, Ebb sensed a sudden hush and stopped to listen. There was no longer the sound of the chase, nor the yelp preluding the treed quarry. Quite some time passed before Ebb heard the frenzied bark begin again. But it came from an unfamiliar place. He ran quickly through the thicket and came into a field of corn, tall and ready for picking. Ebb stopped again, only to hear the rustle of dry corn leaves.

"That Honker. Playin' round and being stubborn, such as the way he is," Ebb thought, and commenced to walk through the corn and into the pine and onward until he came to the edge of an equally unfamiliar clearing. It was Shanty Land. As Ebb recalled:

Honker was sitting at the far end of a little dirt road that came through the town. Jonas was petting him soft. There was three other blacks standin' there, all looking straight down the road at me with their nigger smiles. I suspect there must have been six or seven old houses on both sides of the road. They were sorry looking places. Smelled of fish. None was painted and they looked a pale, gray mouse color. Dried mud was caked to the roofs. Chickens ran in and out the houses. I heard hogs which I suspected was doing some of the same. An old dog sniffed at Honker. But Honker, being frightened, only perked his ears and had nothin' to do with it. He began to whine when he seen me and wagged his tail and tried to pull 'emself loose. But Jonas held Honker tight.

The darkies told Jonas something I couldn't

hear. One I had seen down at the loading dock in Solomons. He had a scar that ran from his right ear clear to his mouth. The two others I never seen before.

I stopped at the edge of the road where I came out of the thicket and called to Honker. But Jonas weren't lettin' 'em go.

"What you doin' with my dog?" I yelled. My voice was so nervous and cracky, I coulda kicked myself.

"We're gonna fuck 'em," Jonas said. They all laughed and chuckled. Scarface made on like he was holdin' something big in his hand.

"You wanta help us fuck 'em?" Jonas said, pleased as you be.

That surprised me and I was about to step back when he said more serious, "Come here, boy!"

I didn't move one inch until he said it again, loud and forceful. A big, fat black man came to the door of one of the shanties and stood silent.

I walked slow toward Jonas. Two black boys, smaller than me, came runnin' up from behind, screamin' and carryin' on. One of 'em jumped on my back and near knocked me over. He held tight around my neck and near choked my head off. He weren't for lettin' go, much as I shook 'em. Ninny on my back, I thought.

He grabbed my ears and pulled 'em somethin' awful. It made 'em all laugh and made me so mad I growled like a mad dog and turned in circles till I got dizzy. Soon as he jumped off my back the other one snuck up and hit my backside with a hard board. It hurt so bad it brung tears to my eyes. I sure wished Grandma was there: She'd kill 'em, I thought. She'd make 'em say "yes ma'am" and "no ma'am." She'd . . .

49

Just then one of the nigger boys whispered some-thin' to Jonas that made him start smilin' again. "White boy fuckin' time," he said out loud, point-ing to me. "Yes, sir, that's what time it is."

No sooner than he said that, I started to run fast as I could but one of the small boys tripped me and before I knowed it, two of the big blacks was hold-ing me tight and threw me to the ground. I knowed I was gonna cry and shook my head something fierce. In less time than it took me to swallow, they had my pants pushed down to my ankles. Black flesh came near. I bit hard and fast and blood ran. Then surprisingly, the two blacks who held me let go and jumped up. Suddenly, niggers was running and leaping in all directions. I thought sure the Lord'd come and was gonna beat 'em all. Then I heard a car engine sounding through the wood, coming closer and closer. Finally I could see an old Pontiac rounding the bend comin' into Shanty. Salt and blood sat in my mouth. I spat like I never spat before. The big Pontiac slid to a halt. An old colored man and two black women stared out the window, ne'er believing what they saw.

"If you got pride, you have the quality, even if the seat of you breeches is out, Ebb Kellum." I thought of what Grandma Kellum always told me.

I remember this warm, summer breeze blowing into Shanty. It felt cool on my thighs. Dust blew up in the dirt road, wound itself in the sunlight and blew amongst the shacks. The big, fat nigger was still standing in the doorway, still starin' at me, mean and silent.

CHAPTER 7

AUTUMN arrived early in that year of 1947. Frost had covered the fields by the second week of September. Ducks and geese had moved steadily south before October ended. The sun set redder, painting the trees more golden each waning day. The scent of the woodlands hung strong and sweet in the fresh, crisp air. Squirrels busily searched for nuts. Rabbits were not to be seen on the byroads anymore. It was the season of the hunt.

Squirrel hunting was one of Ebb's favorite pastimes as well as his favorite time to think. He would sit for hours among the big trees and meditate and feel the stillness. His mind would run free with imagination as he waited patiently for the "bushtail."

It was on such a day that he was down in the woods on the Talbot farm. He had scanned the area prior to hunting season and found the trees replete with squirrel nests. "Full of the biggest squirrels hereabouts— acorn-fat," he declared.

The wind sat still as twilight bled into the horizon— no leaf moved. Ebb sat some thirty yards away, staring into the huge world of a giant oak. Acorns were plentiful and littered the ground. Some were broken and

eaten and some were green on the stumps. The woodland floor was dry—the leaves were cracker crisp. A
solitary bluejay fluttered here and there through the
undergrowth, searching and pecking. Ebb listened intently and claimed to hear the earthworms crawling. It
was calm until the silence was broken by the short,
sharp chatter he had been waiting for. The noise
cocked his senses. Without moving, he searched the
mighty tree, knowing with a hunter's instinct that care-
lessness speaks doom for the hunted. A reddish-yellow
leaf floated slowly down from atop the tree. Then another. Nutshells sprinkled the ground as the luckless
squirrel ate. And then Ebb saw his tail, twitching contentedly high above.

Ebb lifted his 16-gauge double barrel Remington
shotgun up to his chest and slowly pushed the safety
off. The squirrel, once he had finished his meal, moved
quickly along the long narrow branch until he got close
to the tip. He stopped abruptly and hugged the limb,
and waited as if alerted to a danger. It was only an
instinctive measure, however. Ebb knew the moment
well and licked his lips in anticipation as the squirrel
suddenly rose up and sped to his destiny. The thrust of
the animal's body carried him up and across toward
another tree, another branch, when the deafening roar
of the big gun penetrated the woodland silence, cleav-
ing time and space. As if a burst of wind had hit its
agile body from below, the squirrel shot upward, contorted with a searing pain, and then uncontrollably
plunged down toward the earth. He fell flat, through
the branches, plummeting square center onto a last
obstacle to his fall—a large branch some twenty feet
below. The force of the fall bounced him from the
branch. He grasped out in desperation and clung to its
bark. But his uncontrollable weight and waning
strength caused him to slowly lose his hold and fall
heavily to the forest floor.

52

The squirrel still lived and struggled helplessly in the leaves to gain his feet, but his hind legs were broken and lay limp to his task. Ebb saw that it was an old squirrel, grizzled, with a wide, stubby head. It had a full winter coat of shiny gray fur tipped with white. Pellet-holes welled with blood on his hind quarter. As Ebb approached, the squirrel lunged toward him with gnashing teeth, but his front legs carried him nowhere and with frightened eyes he lay alert and ready to fight to the death. The squirrel's body relaxed, but what Ebb had thought to be the throes of death exploded into a last desperate effort to run, to survive. With strenuous, clipped motions, the animal slowly, awkwardly, crawled forward for two feet before the tortured movements caused him to roll futilely onto his back. Frantically moving his head from side to side, the squirrel tried to turn over but to no avail. To stop the animal's suffering, Ebb hit the squirrel in the head with the butt of his gun. The blow stopped the animal's movements momentarily. Its body shuddered, its left eye popped from its socket and blood appeared at the corner of his mouth.

"Please, squirrel, die," Ebb prayed. "I don't mean to hurt ya, you know that." Tears came to Ebb's eyes as he thought to himself. "He's trying so hard to stay alive."

The squirrel lifted his head, as Ebb explained, "like he knowed he was smelling the woods for the last time." The defeated animal finally closed his uninjured eye and lay back slowly in resignation to die. Ebb knelt, took off his shirt and laid it gently over the broken body.

Stunned into an existential fear, Ebb became acutely aware of the reality of death and night. As the hush of darkness settled over the woods, a shadow darker than the night itself came over Ebb and the squirrel. Something breathed steadily. Not Ebb. Not the animal, now.

"God, save!" Ebb repeated fearfully to himself. He turned into the shadow and looked up slowly. Standing tall and ominous in the darkness, someone stared silently, almost respectfully, at Ebb and the squirrel. A burlap bag hung down from his shoulder. Ebb stretched his neck and squinted his eyes. It was Bo.

Bo didn't say a word. He set the bag on the ground, pulled a sap apple from it and held it out for Ebb to take. Ebb felt bashfulness and a kindness in Bo's subtle, hesitant, manner. He took the apple appreciatively. It was speckled and sour, but according to Ebb, tasted better than anything. Bo pulled out another apple for himself. Unmindful of the dark, they sat and ate and stared solemnly at the squirrel.

"Dat's some squirrel," Bo said.

Ebb nodded his head and looked to the sky and a billion stars. The night was cold and bright. Somewhere in the darkness, he heard an owl.

"Good squirrel."

CHAPTER 8

T was after the event of the squirrel hunt that Ebb and Bo became close friends or, as Ebb declared, "real buddies." He considered Bo to have more of the same qualities he had. Bo was adept at undertaking what Ebb called "the ruggedness of the river." He was slender and moved agilely. He could do most anything. He was reticent and listened well. When he spoke, he spoke with honesty. There were no shadows.

Fasso and Top were incensed at Ebb's pursuit of a "nigger's friendship" and took measures to show their resentment. They no longer came over to Ebb's house on Saturday mornings to share in a bounteous meal of Grandma Kellum's oatmeal scones. Nor did they tell Ebb the day's secrets, as was custom among long friends.

In due course, such actions prompted Ebb to take measure of his playmates, especially of Fasso and Topper. Fasso's clumsiness and his vociferous attitudes left nothing more to Ebb's impression than a butch haircut, fleshy arms and rolled-up pants displaying chalk-white scabby knees. Top was "OK," Ebb reflected. Short and thin. Always a follower. Regardless, Ebb liked Top and said that he would always be a friend.

Not that he disliked Fasso entirely. There existed a distant, intuitive allure—a witty, even sadistic appreciation—that linked him to Fasso's forbidden province.

"He's always gettin' in trouble," Ebb declared. "Never allows his ma to catch her breath. . . . But . . . he's that kind, you know. . . ."

Regardless of any excuses or rational measure di rected toward Fasso, indeed, the townspeople considered him to be an ally of the devil. Some even thought him to be tutor to the same.

Ebb recalled Pastor Eves having rushed from his home to call on the Dumblewhites. It must have been a real emergency, for as he was leaving, the pastor had barely pulled his pants to his waist. His black hat teetered on his head. He ran forth tripping several times on his loose shoes and flailing shoestrings. A vociferous denunciation rippled the town's quiet morning coffee as the Dumblewhite house shook with activity, its rumbling reminiscent of earthquake fervor. An exorcising was imminent—if not already at hand.

Up the stairwell Pastor Eves followed the volley of adjurations into Fasso's bedroom. There he found Mrs. Dumblewhite on her knees poking beneath Fasso's bed with a broom handle.

"Come out from under that bed . . . right now! I'm going to have . . ." She looked up at Pastor Eves and in the same exasperated breath expressed her thought.

"Pastor Eves, this boy is of the devil. . . . I'm going to trash this . . ." A rash of fast, misguided thrusts beat against the wall. On the last volley Fasso caught onto the broom handle and held it tightly beneath the bed.

Pastor Eves touched Mrs. Dumblewhite on the shoulder for consolation. Then, as if suddenly imbued with a divine talent for mediation, he held two fingers above his head, and softly said, "God is with you. Let us forgive . . ."

Silence followed his spoken words as Mrs. Dumble-white looked up to the pastor with passionate under-standing and hope.

"Let me persuade the boy," he said solemnly. Full of confidence and good intention he took Mrs. Dumble-white's place. Gingerly he bent over so as to see the boy.

"Fas . . . eh . . . young Kevin . . ." His voice pre-tentious, his words mincing, he resolved to lie flat on the floor to make better visual contact. There he saw a large, beleaguered, bilious lad squeezed under a mere twelve inches of headboard. As a gesture of comforting reassurance, Pastor Eves slid his hand toward Fasso only to withdraw it quickly, having felt Fasso's sudden retaliation. Again and again he tried in vain to persuade young Kevin to take his hand in repentance and for-giveness. Each time he had it kicked or bitten. Finally, losing all sense of dignity and reserve, the pastor grabbed whatever he could of Fasso's quick, fleshy legs. From there the incident proceeded to escalate with impetuous fervor: the bed rocking to and fro, mov-ing up and down; the pastor panting and pulling; Fasso kicking and yelling.

Then, out came one of Fasso's legs with the pastor holding fast! But no sooner than victory seemed almost certain, the pastor was quickly jerked back toward the bed. His head and shoulders disappeared again be-neath the springs. Once more there was a tumultuous display of kicking and panting. As quickly as it had begun, it was over. Pastor Eves lay still and breathless.

"Oh, my God!" Mrs. Dumblewhite cried. Quickly she took hold of the pastor's legs and awkwardly pulled him from beneath the bed.

"Are you all right?"

The Reverend Mr. Eves could only grunt and hold his mouth in shocked astonishment and mounting fury. Mrs. Dumblewhite noticed blood dribbling down the sides of his mouth. Again, she picked up the broom and was about to commence poking beneath the bed. Suddenly, the pastor stood up, and with a mighty fury, hurled the mattress off the bed.

Fasso, now crouched in a fetal position, glanced innocently up through the bedsprings. Lithely he turned onto his back and clung tightly to the bedsprings, forcibly adding to the weight of the four-poster bed and thereby prohibiting Mrs. Dumblewhite and the pastor from moving the bed in any way.

Mrs. Dumblewhite proceeded to beat each fat finger that clung to the springs with the broom handle, while the pastor attempted to pry loose Fasso's tenacious grip. But the resolute boy desperately held on to the bedsprings, forcing the pastor and Mrs. Dumblewhite to take the bed apart—piece by piece.

The issue was never resolved nor even discussed. Whatever had occurred was no doubt too horrendous or too personal to admit to or to disclose. Never had there been a thrashing more profound or a backside more sore than Fasso's when he finally emerged from his house that day. He had to stand up in school for the whole following week. Fasso, however, was a protagonist to the very end and the events that followed are still talked about with amusement and incredulity. Call it a tit-for-tat or an-eye-for-an-eye; the pastor and Fasso continued their "battle" with unflagging fury.

Fewer than three weeks had passed before Fasso once again unleashed his vengeance. Absorbed in the care and curing of a still very sore rear end, Fasso walked leisurely along Perch Way with his dog, Spy, a mongrel of mastiff lineage, a bully and a terror to "lesser" animals—especially cats. As fate would have it, both boy and dog simultaneously saw the Reverend Mr. Eves's prized cat, a narcissistic Persian of reputed pedigree and a blue ribbon winner at the Prince Frederick county fair. Seeing the dog, the cat scurried up the nearest tree—a large maple—and observed, with apparent amusement and obvious self-assurance, the frustrated mongrel. Not wasting a moment, Fasso revengefully shinnied himself slowly and determinedly up the tree trunk, pursuing the pastor's cat to the very top of the tree. The cat screamed in terror as Fasso grabbed it off the highest branch, dragged the helpless animal by the tail back down the tree and held the terrified creature aloft.

"Here, boy. C'mon. Kitty, kitty. Got somethin' fo' ya. . . . Boy. . . . Here, boy. . . ."

Spy leaped high with excitement. The cat clawed the useless air. As the anxious bark of the dog became more frenzied, Fasso dropped the cat. Its legs outstretched, its back arched in terror, fur and fang unfurled in a screaming torrent that would leave the neighbors to shake with the memory.

It was at the following Sunday church service that all was disclosed. Fasso was made to stand before the congregation as Pastor Eves, his two front teeth missing, denounced in a quivering voice Kevin "Fasso" Dumblewhite for displaying characteristics unnatural to "civilized mankind" and for killing "one fine cat."

Ebb and Bo hunted hard that winter. The black ducks and canvasbacks were plentiful. The geese were big and fat, and graced the sky in large conversant flocks. In the evenings, they would appear as phantom birds stretched out across the river's horizon, sailing the sky as they caressed the air waves with their great wings in search of a refuge in the calm estuaries. At times a golden sun reflected on their backs, heralding the winter solstice, happy there are geese. Wood ducks whistled by, pursuing instinct. The divers paid little heed.

At times Ebb and Bo would roast a duck or goose at the edge of the sawgrass while they sat in silence and watched the fading sunset. Hypnotic reds and yellows and oranges. Glimmering. Ebb's dog, Honker, pleased his mind and watched the birds fly high.

"He'd sit there for hours if we'd let 'em," Ebb said. "Once he even froze. We had to carry 'em back to the house and thaw out his bones. That's the way Patuxent sunsets is. When it all fades away into the night, you gotta shake your head and wake up your senses. Either way, you sorry when it's over."

One day, a swan flew slowly over their hunting blind. The graceful bird stood out big and white against the bleak, stormy sky. After much reflection, Bo said, "White's pretty, ain't it?"

Ebb nodded his head in agreement. After a pause, and with a sudden subconscious impulse, he replied much to his surprise, "Bo, I'm glad you ain't a nigger."

Bo looked with bewilderment at Ebb. He squinted his eyes in disbelief. Uncertain of what Ebb had said, he repeated, "Not a nigger?"

"No, you ain't a nigger," Ebb assured him. Startled by this sudden revelation, Ebb shuddered at this consciousness of thought. This force so subtle, apathetic. Unleashed in innocence, Ebb suddenly understood a lurking malignancy of the human mind—a great vulnerability. In embarrassment, he waited.

Bo scratched his head, and said hesitantly, "Yeah, I guess you right. But people call me a nigger sometimes."

"Is that right!" Ebb stretched his arms and squirmed uncomfortably on his seat.

"I got called a dirty, mother-fuckin' nigger once," Bo accented.

"Who called you that?"

"Some nigger."

"Well, that's not bad. I mean, you ain't if you ain't."
Ebb hesitated and, with euphemism, responded, "Even
if you are, those gooses up there got dark meat. They's
the kings of the air. Nobody calls 'em nigger gooses!
You don't hear 'em frettin' none. They glide in straight
and powerful, always knowing where they're goin'.
. . . Anyway, whoever told you that is the worst thing
. . . I mean telling you something and you go on believing it; even for your whole life. If somebody told you I
was a muskrat and you believed 'em, and then they told
you they gonna trap muskrat, you'd think they gonna
trap me. Ain't that right?"

"Now, who gonna believe dat?" Bo looked at Ebb
with amusement.

"Ain't you ever learned somethin' that ain't true?"
Ebb asked. "Remember that story about Little Red
Riding Hood and the Wolf?"

Bo shook his head. "No, I ain't," he said matter-of-
factly. He stood up and pretended not to listen.

As silly as Ebb felt, he told Bo the story and when he
had finished, said, "Now, you know there ain't a wolf
in this world that's smart enough to put a hat on and
get in bed and talk. Red Ridin' Hood saying, 'Hi,
Granny! How you all doing?' "

At that, both Ebb and Bo broke into hearty laughter
and rolled playfully in the snow.

CHAPTER 9

T was only after such interludes that Ebb
came to understand the intrinsic attitudes associated
with being "socially accepted." Margie Kellum had
given Ebb explicit instructions at some time in his life
not to play with black people or associate with or have
any dealings with "their kind." Even though he
couldn't remember exactly when such instruction was
given, he often felt that the subtle inference pervaded
Solomons' daily manner. The pressures of being called
a "nigger lover" and "no friend" by his contemporaries
deeply angered Ebb and spurred his independent nature. "Disrespect" was the way Ebb saw it and, however sensitive his feelings, Ebb shunned the atavistic
fear which burdened his peers.

It was in the summer of that year that Ebb was
moved to resolve. What Ebb would have thought to be
a travesty of human weakness was now measured as an
undeniable flaw in man's search for human integrity.

The incident took place when the multifaceted Her-
cules stood firm in the northern sky and the great August moon rose full with the flood tide. Ebb and Bo
watched its great orb solemnly fill the eastern horizon
and move slowly along its celestial axis. They fished

the edge of the deep, sandy channel adjacent to the plankton-rich shoals off Sandy Point. The pungent smell of citronella and kerosene tinged the still night air, and other than the deep shadow cast by the light of the ascending moon and the occasional whisk of phosphorescent light of disturbed larvae surrounding the periphery of their boat, only the single flame of a rusty Coleman lamp told the river that they were there.

Bo held a hand line. He regularly moved the heavy string up and down to attract the fish and at times jerked the fishing line vehemently to dissuade the abundant nibblers. Likewise Ebb fished on the leeward side. Three large perch and an eel occasionally flopped and slid on the wet deck. The expectation of catching a lot of fish was now remote, since they had used up their peeler bait. Only the remains of a single big Jimmie crab lay sectioned on the gunwale.

Having little success, Ebb pulled in his line to check his bait and, on seeing his two hooks full of hard crab meat, lowered his line once again to the bottom and secured it to the oarlock. He then lay across the stern board of the boat and stared into the pitch black water. His mind imagined a monstrous shark staring up at him from beneath the surface. The spell was broken when his attention was drawn to the diaphanous umbrella of a jellyfish as it waltzed wondrously through the sparkling plankton, its numerous tentacles caressing its shifting domain.

Bo, observing Ebb's more relaxed position, likewise tied his fishing line to a forward stay and lay back in the bow in comfort. They both enjoyed the remoteness and, after the last muted shifting of their positions, studied the heavens with stilled awe.

Ten minutes passed without incident. Even the sudden rock of their boat went unnoticed as Bo's fishing line slowly drew out and became taut. Not simply taut,

63

but a seizure drawn up and out with unmitigated strength. Both boys unconsciously watched the constellations move from left to right as their skiff swung about. Only on feeling the heavy yawing of their boat did they realize that something was askew.

"Bo, your line! It's your line!"

Bo grabbed the tight fishing line. It would not budge. The boat shuddered as the great force below increased its speed.

"It's gonna sink the boat! What we gonna do?" Bo avoided the line and stepped back in fright. Ebb grabbed the cleaning knife and quickly cut the anchor rope.

"We ain't lettin' it go, that's for sure," Ebb said excitedly.

The great power stopped at the unleashing of the big weight from above. The line fell slack. Disheartened, Ebb jumped to the bow and felt the line. Foot by foot he weighed its length.

"We lost 'em." No longer taking measure, he pulled the fishing line in hurriedly when they heard something break the surface of the river with great anger, and in the distance they saw the glow of something huge. The line snapped from Ebb's hand and became taut once again, drawing the boat to port, lunging it forward as the great power sounded and steadily moved toward the bay towing the skiff behind it. Both boys sat in wonder as they realized the great size of their quarry.

"Do you think it's a shark?" Bo fearfully asked.

Ebb shook his head. "A shark," he repeated. "I don't know. There ain't nothing that big here."

An hour had passed when they realized that the boat was slowing down. Ebb tested the tightness of the line. It was more relaxed. They waited and as the boat came to a lull, Ebb began to pull the fishing line in slowly. There was little weight until he had drawn in four feet of the line. The resistance grew, but was now manageable. Ebb motioned to Bo, and they both fearfully pulled the mighty burden in slowly toward their boat. Ebb recalled that at each pull they expected to meet their doom and were sure of it when the deep resonant drumming sound of their mysterious catch erupted beneath their feet. Staring down into ink-black water they stopped their motion and held expectantly to the fishing line when they saw rising slowly from the depths a great fish, longer than the boat itself, its massive body aglow in the larva fields of the Chesapeake. The cold, expressionless eye of the giant fish stared at Ebb and then, on seeing the boat, it plunged to the depths once again, following its instinct to retreat to the sanctuary of the great ocean. But its energies were spent. Its gills no longer functioned in balance and propulsion. The big fish was drowning.

Slowly, watchfully—with careful, steadfast determination—Ebb and Bo pulled the weary fish to the surface. Upon its surrender, they both stood gaping at its magnificent size. Its drumming filled the night with the deep timbre of the channel bass. The coarse, raw crab bait still held to the 7/0 hook. The hook's shank was bent slightly but its twin barb held fast above the maxillary bone of the fish's upper jaw.

"How we gonna get 'em in?" Bo asked. "He's tired."

"We can't get 'em in. He's too big. Look, he's bigger than the boat." They pulled the fish closer to the skiff and once they were sure that the fish was tame, Bo tied a loop around his tail while Ebb hooked his line to the fish's mouth and worked an additional hemp line through its gill slit and up and out through the fish's mouth. They secured the big fish to the side of the boat and with boyish candor shook hands for a job well done. Joyously they rowed back toward the Patuxent River and Sandy Point, all the while keeping a watchful eye on their prized catch. However tiring, the thrill of the moment superseded any complaints.

"He's a record, I know!" Ebb said enthusiastically. "Look at his size! What you say, a hundred pounds?"

Bo shook his head in agreement and said, "It's big."

"Boy, when we get to Solomons and they see this fish . . . Bo, you goin' to be famous."

Bo stared at Ebb with surprise and apprehension. After a long minute of silence, he said with determination, "It's your fish, not mine."

With perplexed emotion, Ebb squinted his eyes. "Mine?" He continued to stare at Bo and once convinced that Bo was sincere, he said, "Bo, it's your fish! It was on your line. You caught it. You pulled it in!"

"You pulled it in, too."

"We both pulled it in, but you caught it. Don't you wanta be famous? You'll be the biggest, most well known fisherman there is. Don't you wanta be that?"

Bo hung his head and reluctantly said, "No."

"Why not? I would. He's the biggest . . ."

"You do it. I don't want the fish."

"But Bo . . ." Dawn was breaking to the east. It was slack tide. The air was warm and sweet. They could now see Solomons Island and were rowing toward its harbor.

"Please don't take the fish there," Bo pleaded.

"Why not?" Ebb was indeed perplexed.

"I don't want it. You leave me off somewhere and you take it in."

"Bo, I don't know what . . ."

"Please," Bo said emphatically. He turned his face away toward the fish and said nothing more.

"Don't you want people to see?" Ebb insisted. Dismayed, Ebb steadied the boat and with a flip of his starboard oar turned the skiff toward Crow's Landing, the closest promontory to be seen which was nearest their respective homes. They rowed in silence and on

66

approaching shore Ebb jumped out of the boat and guided the boat to shore.

They untied the fish and laid him on the beach. Ebb shook his head once again and in disbelief said, "It sure is big."

Bo was noticeably more agreeable, whereby Ebb took the opportunity to improve the moment. He turned to Bo.

"How much do you weigh?"

" 'Bout ninety pounds, I guess, at least that's what my ma says."

Ebb lifted Bo up under his arms. By comparison, he then lifted the fish up by the gills with both hands, barely able to hold it to his chin.

"It weighs more than you," he assured Bo.

They dragged the fish further up on the shore and sat and marveled at its size. Its scales were coin size to a quarter and reminded Ebb of the giant carcass of a fish he had seen on the same shores two years previously.

"What we gonna do with 'em?" Ebb asked directly.

They stared at the fish for minutes more, when Bo said again, "You take 'em. I don't want 'em."

"But Bo, we . . ."

"I can't. I's just a nigger."

"What you mean, you can't . . ." Suddenly Ebb saw the humiliation of suppressed joy in Bo's anxious eyes.

Tired and dismayed, they left the fish where it lay and did not return until the late afternoon. Vultures hopped irritably back and forth avoiding the lapping river. The great fish carcass, half eaten, gave way inch by inch to the increasing ebb and gradually floated off into the river and its mysterious depths. Subconsciously, Ebb now knew the plight of the pariah.

CHAPTER 10

I T was at the old ship grave at Bluegeon Slough where much thought was given the subject. The barnacled remnants of a certain skipjack galley interested Ebb. Its hull was bedecked with a mat of Lincoln-green moss, the periphery of which was skeletal and a harbor for a variety of sea life. It was hidden well amongst the open debris and gave access only by an arduous, muddy, undefined path extending from a seemingly untrodden shore out into the brackish slough by approximately thirty yards. At high tide, only the most adventurous, inquiring sort would dare approach such an obstacle; that is, unless they came by boat. And why should they? The wreck resembled nothing to the wandering eye but another dying epoch. It was here that Ebb industriously set out to establish a secret club, reserved for specially selected, Patuxent River club members. With that priority in mind, he immediately commenced to haul driftwood out on the flood tide and to patch up his clubhouse with mud and seaweed and to make it comfortable for at least two privileged members. The improvised room became dark and, by Ebb's standards, even comfortable.

Inspired by his progress, Ebb thought it would be

fitting and proper to have a log book and an official club name. In due course, he quickly resolved both. For the log book, he chose an old, dusty brown book cover which he had often seen in his attic. The book was a gilt-edged album, engraved with the gold initials "C.M.K." on a suede leather covering. A small gold-faced lock embellished its cover, useless and broken. Ebb set it on a small scrap of table in the clubhouse and filled it with Margie Kellum's writing paper. Ebb described the book once it was complete as having an air of elegance and looking "rich," the kind of book that held important matters.

As to the club name, that took much thinking. After a night and two full days and the completion of the clubhouse, he recalled the story of the infamous Black-beard and his exciting buccaneer ways. With such thoughts in mind, he immediately sat down and wrote in his log book as fast as he could remember:

1. Mr. Blackbeard is an honor member of the club.
2. The club name from this day on is the Blackbeard —Ebb Club.
3. Who ever else came a club member can put their name there too.

On the next day Ebb brought Bo out to the club-house. Excited by the secrecy of the event, Bo's fanta-sies touched on everything he saw. With solemn wonder, he sat on the uneven floor of the small room and looked to Ebb with exalted respect.

"You wanta belong to the club, don't you, Bo?" Ebb's voice was firm and serious and intentional. Bo nodded his head enthusiastically. The word "secret" was expressed as tantamount to the deepest honor. Ebb emphasized the necessity to exclude "niggers, Germans and Japs" and explained how he, Bo, would have

69

to do "certain things" before he became a member. Then with dramatic aplomb, he announced the membership of Blackbeard.

"He's gonna give us a secret book, 'most sacred as the Bible, 'specially for us."

Bo's demeanor was remarkably calm at this juncture, but on the declaration that Bo, once he was made a member of the club, would have his name added to the club's name, he burst out into an aura of happiness and revolved three times on the seat of his pants, all the while quacking like a duck. The next day he brought food and certain condiments to the club and asked Ebb a million times about when they were going to meet Blackbeard.

It wasn't long after their first club meeting that Ebb gave full consideration to the drafting of club procedure and those things which would add certain interest and communal flair. His search in the attic had produced a picture book describing flags, animal tracks and such. He tore out the pages of the animal tracks and placed them in an envelope and wrote in large, black letters:

MR. EBB KELLUM AND CLUB MEMBERS

Beneath the writing, he wrote in red letters the word *ONLY*.

The next day, he reported to Bo that a letter, official and most important, was to arrive every Monday from Mr. Blackbeard and that a club book was to be kept containing such letters. It was on this premise that Ebb snuck to the hut and carefully hid the weekly letter. Each Monday morning Bo anxiously crawled into the club room.

"You think he come today, Ebb?"

Bo would look around the room, hoping to catch a glimpse of the message before Ebb. But Ebb's timing always precluded any haphazard investigation. With due process Ebb informed Bo of the intuitive ability of a club member to read clues and find messages. Accordingly, Ebb searched in the shadows. He scratched on the boards, all the while chanting an imaginative incantation. When the time was appropriate, as if startled by some indescribable insight, Ebb crouched cautiously to the spot and pointed excitedly to the place where he had concealed the "sacred bundle." Bo, all this time, as Ebb described, would "look harder than a worm-catchin' bird." He would shake his head and pretend to see the same. Ebb would retrieve the letter and hold it up for Bo's eyes to say, "You sure is somethin', Ebb Kellum!"

It wasn't long after three such episodes that Ebb told Bo that if he ever found the secret message before Ebb did, according to the rules of the club and by a decree of Blackbeard himself, Bo could graduate and become a most honorary member.

According to Ebb, the occasion was to be so splendid that he had to have a document more sacred than his own life, and so thinking, focused all of his efforts on the ultimate prize—The Kellum Letter.

Ebb had seen the letter only once, five years back. At that time a commotion had taken place upon its arrival. Margie Kellum and his Uncle Elton had read it several times whereupon they placed it in the family Bible and locked it in Margie's cedar chest. She told Ebb of its importance and instructed him that he should not "meddle" with it until he was "old enough." Nothing more was ever said.

On the appointed day, Bo arrived early and by design, Ebb came late. When he climbed down the portal, Bo had already lit a candle and was sitting silently in the shadows. Only his face reflected the brightness of the flames and as Ebb explained, "He looked like he had a sunball in his mouth." Ebb immediately pretended to look for the hidden letter. Bo had patted everything back in place and didn't leave any signs of his intrusion. Ebb crawled to the spot where he had hidden the letter and uncovered the hiding place.

"I got some kind of strange feelin', Bo!" Ebb said and in turning found Bo proudly holding the letter high over the candlelight. Ebb grabbed Bo and hugged him in earnest.

"God blessed, Bo! You's one of the club! You done passed the first time!"

Bo carried the letter around and around the candle and hugged it to his bosom. They both sat down again and observed the envelope closely. "Be special careful with it, Bo," Ebb said. "Extra special careful!" Bo gently handed the letter to Ebb.

The letter was addressed to Mr. Elton Kellum, Solomons Island, Maryland. Someone had written in pencil on the back of the envelope the words "St. Lô, France, July 1943." Ebb opened the envelope slowly and, with solemn process, held the letter closer to the candle. Taking a deep breath, he commenced to read each word as if it was a prayer:

Dear Brother,

As we expect orders to march on the enemy every minute I take this opportunity to drop you a few lines. I received the pictures 2 or 3 days ago, also the newspapers which I distributed around the tents. They were received with many thanks by our boys and very generally read by them. The country news I have read through with pleasure. I have been unwell for a day or two but nothing serious yet. I have been excused from duty but I will go tomorrow or when we start whenever it is if I can get one leg before the other. The boys are in good spirits and eager to get into an engagement with the enemy. And although the question is asked once in a while who of us will come back, it is answered cheerfully in somewhat the following manner: "It don't make much difference with me if I die in service of my country and I die a glorious death." We have truly a company of patriots who fight for and are willing to die for its benefit.

Ebb and Bo looked at each other momentarily with surprise. Ebb continued:

Elton, if I should fall in battle and my body can be recovered, it will be sent to you by express—and I want it laid beside the rest of the family. I feel that it is useless for me to request you to do it for I know that it will be done without. Give my respects to all the friends and especially to the family. Write to me as soon as you can. Direct your letters to:

PVT. Chase M. Kellum
A.P.O. New York 09108

—and they will come direct to me. I have not seen anything of that line from Ezra in your letter, but I suppose it is on account of your writing so late at night.

Give my love to Mother and tell her that although I have been a wayward boy, I still remember her as my best friend. I have been "the creature of circumstances" and I feel that in many things I have done wrong, but that is past. Take good care of my son. He is most of what I think of and deeply love. I will now bid you good-bye. Write when ever you can and remember me as your loving Brother,

Chase

P.S. I sure miss the hunting and fishing. Send me some pictures of your catch. By the way Brother, I forgive you for shooting my beagle. I never told you this, but I thought it was a rabbit at the time, also.

At the bottom of the letter was written—"Please turn over. A letter to my Son." Ebb turned it over with more interest than observation and continued to read:

Dear Son:

I received the picture of you. You are a handsome boy and a right notable fisherman for the size of that hardhead

73

you caught. It must weigh at least five pounds from what I can tell.

You and me are going to catch a lot of those big ones when I get home. I want . . .

Ebb abruptly stopped reading. For the first time in his life he was overcome by remorse. A deep sorrow for those elusive thoughts now prevailed and controlled the moment. Distant and esoteric, its ethereal presence embodied a goodness and a happiness from his past. A forgotten past. An infant past. To lie on a threshold of another dimension. A past barely touched or understood, only to be fed and forgiven, and in time to be respected. Ebb told of a strange silence—a vision that followed his finishing that letter:

> I saw in the flickering of the candlelight Chase Kellum, Sr. He stood as serious as anything, and when he went to open his mouth to speak, he exploded into a giant, fearsome jellyfish what danced slowly with the tide. Then that too exploded, only bigger. Weird red river water reached high into the sky and became silver wasps—millions of 'em screaming to the sea—'Tissssssssssssssssss . . . !
>
> Bo swept past me like a lightning bolt. I weren't for waitin' either and jumped out of that hull as fast as I could.
>
> "D'you blow out that candle?" I said to Bo. I was sure scared. Bo shook his head, no, and said, "Maybe it dat creature of 'stances." I couldn't agreed with him more.

Ebb deeply felt the qualms of guilt and explained to Bo that it was necessary to return this special letter to its sacred place of rest as Blackbeard had instructed. He did so with august devotion.

74

CHAPTER 11

EBB and Bo met at the clubhouse often. The fall swept by in a flood of activity as did much of the winter and by the time February arrived they had several new trot lines prepared and laid neatly and tucked closely in wicker baskets. Fish hooks were sharpened, and a special big fish rig hung neatly from the wall displaying a six-inch tuna hook and one hundred and twenty feet of seasoned hemp rope. A large Gulf oil drum sat outside the galley and floated on the tides attached securely to the upper rafters, ready and fitted out to wear on that "demon of the deep."

In anticipation of the spring, Ebb jumped from bed each morning and searched from his window for a sure sign of that marvel he loved most in nature's way. It wasn't until mid-March that he saw his first sign. "Daffodils popped up before my eyes," he described. "They made a carpet of yellow, the likes I rarely seen across the fields of snow. In time a million robins was suddenly there, chirpin' and pickin' worms off the lawn. It sent a magic wind that brought the smell of fishin' to the air. The Patuxent ribbons stretched their way to the Chesapeake Bay. The ice disappeared as fast as it came and boats started coming out on the water more each day. Everybody'd be waving and askin', 'How you been all winter?' The gardens were spaded up and made ready for sowing. No more quilts, no more knickers, no more shoes." According to Ebb, even school was tolerable.

Sister Edwards had started a contest in which each student was to bring in samples of nature for class study. The "best" and the "most" was to receive a prize each of a silver St. Christopher medal. Such was play for Ebb, and with Bo's assistance he went hunting in the plowed corn fields and found arrowheads and many lesser, not-so-distinct artifacts. One day Bo dug up a skull that was indeed suspicious looking. He and Ebb carried it carefully to the clubhouse and examined it closely.

"We got us a dinosaur, you know?" Ebb said seriously. Bo jumped back from the skull as Ebb turned it over with a small stick.

"What you do that for?" Ebb asked. "Ain't you ever seen a dinosaur before?"

The skull had deteriorated to where only the jaw and three large teeth remained intact, the resemblance of which reminded Ebb of Miss Agnus Fannon with her buck teeth. Upon further examination, Ebb suggested that the skull might be a horse skull instead. Bo, however, insisted that it couldn't be because it looked too mean. Thereupon, they indeed both agreed that it was a dinosaur and marked it as such with a red crayon, and hung it in a place of prominence on the wall.

Now that Bo was a true member of the club he was assured that he would no longer be ridiculed as "a nigger" or "any association" thereof. Ebb stated that such respect truly warranted a new club name and so in due course, a new name was established—B.E.B. —Blackbeard, Ebb and Bo. The name was considered good and most appropriate by the unanimous vote of

76

two enthusiastic "yeas" whereupon Ebb wrote in the club log that from that day forth anybody coming into the club must say the passwords "BEB, BEB, BEB, BEB"—and such was protocol. The secrecy of the club was well established until one day Ebb heard a familiar voice echo out over the slough.

"Chase!"

It was Margie Kellum's voice. Ebb unplugged the peephole and looked out. Hardly believing his eyes, he saw her rowing slowly but steadily in their direction. There was a strap laid neatly across the centerboard seat. Ebb motioned to Bo to blow out the candle. Margie stopped rowing and hollered "Chase" again. Scared as they were, they didn't move a hair. The next time they heard her call, she was right next to the wreck. Her skiff smacked into the old hull and jolted it, sending loose dirt and sand to sift down between the narrow cracks. Barnacles fell off into the water. Ebb looked out of the hole again. Everything looked black. He blinked his eyes and looked again. It was still black. Then he heard heavy breathing and suddenly realized that he was looking square into Margie Kellum's eyeball.

"Chase, are you in there? Chase!" she called again. Ebb hesitantly looked into the hole once more and much to his relief, he saw daylight once again. They heard her mumble something to herself and saw her finally row off in another direction, praying to the Lord for Ebb's resurrection. They couldn't help but snicker.

"Ain't no place more hidden than this one," Ebb whispered proudly. "Blackbeard sure gave us the good plans." Ebb could tell Bo was smiling big, and glad he had joined the club.

After that episode, the hideaway wasn't safe anymore. It wasn't that they didn't take the proper precautions. The procedure for secrecy was followed without fault. The trouble arose when Fasso and Top refused to wait their turn to join the club.

"We got to have a proper sign for admittin' anybody more," Ebb explained to them. "The log says it's three in the club and that's all that's allowed for now." He was quite emphatic.

Fasso and Top got mad and said that for letting a nigger in first, Ebb was a "traitor" and a "dirty, rotten shithead." They threatened to tell everybody about the hideout. And they did.

A short time after Margie Kellum's visit, Ebb and Bo found the clubhouse hatch stick laid aside, and the trap door ajar. On opening the portal, a repulsive odor stifled the air. The room appeared empty, but on lighting the candle Ebb saw that Tedor Rabbin, Fasso's brother, had been there. He explained that Tedor always "left a pile of 'emself so's you know he's been visiting." It wasn't long after that that Ebb and Bo sought a new refuge and came to settle for Slough Hen Cove.

CHAPTER 12

LOUGH Hen Cove is a big cove. When the tide changes, one could believe that its outlet is a river in itself; its tidal flow is fast and steady and in many places very deep. Not many people come to this spot because of its treacherous currents and its rapid, indeterminate excavation of sand banks. However, within its confines it was peaceful. Ebb and Bo felt the joy of solitude and a place to come to.

Ebb and Bo would sit for hours on its sand bank and watch the tide move in and out of its narrow gate. On a calm day when the flood rose high on its shore, the atmosphere of the inlet became very quiet and still. At times they could see clearly to the bottom of its deepest chasm. Sudden globular swirls of tidal water would mysteriously boil up from beneath and burst out onto its flowing surface in smooth, expansive, orbicular patterns only to dissolve slowly and disappear into the distant calm.

The parade of the day commencing with each tide would feature the minnows as they swam casually with the current, determined and anxious to follow the leader, unaware of the stalking danger of the marsh hens who sat in the shallows, waiting silently for their meal. Then came the crabs. One. Two. Sometimes as many as three or four at a time crawled slowly on the gravel bed and approached the sanctuary as if on a family picnic. There would be busters and shedders, the soft and the hard. Even doublers arrived, tenderly embraced. At times a crab would wander too close to the central current and be caught up in its force and speed off past the others, its appendages spread wide and stabilized for the free ride. When the river reached full flood, the big fish moved in; the shedders turned soft; the marsh birds moved high and the cove became an arena of the hunter and the hunted. Sometimes the boys would sight a muskrat gliding leisurely beneath the surface. There was something fine about a muskrat, Ebb recalled. He described them as "peaceful, bashful sorts; true seamen."

Ebb and Bo liked the cove better than the old boat galley. The only inconvenience was that they didn't have a clubhouse. But it wasn't long before they thought of the ultimate structure—an underground fort.

"That's what Blackbeard'll want. I know," Ebb said. At the ebb they were able to climb over the huge trunk of a fallen oak tree to the opposite side of the cove's entrance, to a short, narrow bank of land. On surveying the site, they declared it perfect for the new clubhouse. The location was accessible only at the low tide due to the treacherous current which swept its shore. A steep cliff entangled with what seemed an impenetrable jungle of vines and undergrowth acted as a natural portico to its rear. The site was well hidden. The earth was porous and easy to manage, and in three days they had completed a most suitable and secret hideaway, so secret, Ebb claimed, that once it was completed they had trouble finding the opening. Bo found a dried-up toadfish and stuck it on the end of a stick. He stuck the

80

pole into the ground and walked back to where Ebb could see him.

"Dat's so ya can tell where we is!" he shouted. Then he ran back and said, "Ya can't see it if you ain't close."

Ebb ran back to where Bo had come from and looked curiously in the direction of the stick. Sure enough, Ebb couldn't see it either, without straining his eyesight, and told Bo that he was "right smart." They then commenced to make a door covering out of sawgrass, pine branches and driftwood. When they finished, they laid it on top of the opening and sat back and looked at it for a long time when Bo said, "How you gonna tell if anybody's in it?"

"Who's gonna be in it, 'ceptin' you and me?" Ebb said.

"Spirits!" Bo emphasized.

Such thoughts had never occurred to Ebb until then. He got up slowly and walked thoughtfully toward the thatched door covering. "Anybody down there?" Ebb called jokingly. He shrugged his shoulders and turned to Bo. "The toad pole'll scare the spirits, won't it?" he asked.

Bo said maybe, but that they had to make sure and that the only way was to put the toad pole inside the fort. "I ain't goin' down there first, though," Bo assured him. Ebb backed off.

Finally after much indecision, Ebb took the pole and pushed it forcefully through the top of the hut so that it easily went up and down. He pulled it back and forth several times and stomped his feet. "There," he said. "There ain't no spirits now!" Ebb crawled cautiously to the doorway and slid it back carefully. He looked with apprehension down into the dark hole. After lighting a candle, he jumped in and hurriedly pushed up the toad pole. "Ya see it?" he hollered to Bo.

81

"Yeaaaaaah, man! I see it!" Bo said excitedly and jumped down into the hut. That same day, they wrote in the log book:

Spirits—and chasing the spirits:
      —walk three steps from the toad-pole.
      —signal with foot three times.
      —signal with foot three more times.

CHAPTER 13

L IFE on Solomons Island was a happy and eventful one for Ebb and now that he enjoyed Bo's companionship there was added a richer, more diverse dimension, a frontier of profound implication and a world of new challenge. A new vision. Only the usual nuisances prevailed, such as the mosquitoes on a still summer night and, when the necessity arose, going to the outhouse on a cold winter day. When the snows came, the path to the privy always iced over.

"If you ever stepped off the walk just once," Ebb tells, "you got a shoe a snow. Nobody ever killed 'emselves slipping that I knowed of, but my Uncle Ezra come near doing it many times. I always watched 'em 'cus he took the slide like he's walking a tightrope, you know, on his tiptoes. That's his way, slow and careful. Sometimes he'd rock back on his heels. His legs would bow and near give out. His arms most often shot out in all directions. If you didn't know 'em, you'd sure think his manner a bit peculiar."

The "honey-house," the euphemistic term used in these parts for a shit-house (and even *that* might be considered euphemistic depending on your status), was set far enough from the main house so that it wasn't considered too far, but far enough that a stranger wouldn't notice its presence. The structure was built from old pine barnboards turned gray from age and weather. Inside, the rudiments of comfort were afforded—an oaken seat carved to fit the most adequate posterior, and a makeshift toilet paper spool which hung loosely by a clothes hanger, its utilization limited to being a handy place to hang old Sears catalogue paper. The toilet seat was worn smooth and well preserved. This wooden shell of an outhouse was moved atop a newly dug hole every two years.

When Ebb sat inside the honey-house he claimed he could see everything that was going on outside due to the undisputed fact that there were a thousand knotholes. One day as Ebb sat on the "pot" looking out of one of these knotholes, he realized that nothing would stop anyone from looking in and seeing everything that was going on inside if they looked through the knotholes from the outside. That day he decided to test his theory. On contributing his due to the infernal pyramid, he went outside to the back of the privy and snuck slowly up to the shack to take a look. He put his eye to the first knothole he came to and busily strained his sight to see what he could see. Suddenly a firm hand grabbed him hard by his ear. It was Margie Kellum.

Ebb tried to explain to his grandmother that it was pitch black inside and that he couldn't see anything and that there was nobody inside the outhouse anyhow.

"Look inside," he motioned eagerly. "Go ahead. There's nobody there!"

She refused. According to Kellum standards, she said, it was "certainly no noble deed to be looking into the knotholes of an outhouse whether anyone was there or not. And if there *was* someone . . ." She stopped short and grabbed Ebb by his ear again and led him into the house. As Ebb related, "I got thrashed for seeing things I ain't ever seen yet."

84

Ebb liked the seclusion of the privy. There he would imitate Blackbeard or recite his poem, say anything he pleased as loud as he wished. From the main house, any oratory was indiscernible to the casual ear. The opportunity encouraged Ebb's undeniable talent for blarney.

It was also quiet and peaceful, so quiet at times that the silence amplified many of the subtleties of nature, such as the unseen diffusion of ice splintering on the river ice floe in winter or the monotonous drone of a casual fly or, as Ebb would imagine, the spirits moving sullenly below.

Even the spiders added an archaic, forbidden charm, their high-hanging webs displaying a colorful array of insects, some of which floated precariously above, secured only by a single strand of a silky net. Ebb fondly remembered one spider he named "Majesty." It was the biggest and blackest of all the spiders and always had the most food.

"Every time I'd come in," Ebb fondly remembers, "he came peeking out just to make sure I knew he was there. Just before I'd leave, I'd find something he could eat and drop it in his net. In the winter time, he would disappear. I couldn't blame 'em. It'd get so cold, my breath'd near freeze. You couldn't sit for long 'cus your bones would stick to the seat. But come spring, sittin' was good and there my friend would be. It sure made me glad."

The winter of 1949 was colder than most. It snowed heavily and often. The Patuxent River froze over and Periwinkle Pier was uprooted and stood high on the naked ice. Open water was hard to find. At times, Ebb and Bo searched as far as the Chesapeake Bay before they came to a break in its surface.

It was on such an occasion that Ebb and Bo spotted a waterhole over an oyster bed belonging to Mr. Poe. Laboriously, they dragged tide boards and a pair of

85

oyster tongs to the site. Ebb placed the boards carefully around the hole while Bo set the heaviest and broadest board on top and across the deep blue pool. Since Ebb had had experience in tonging oysters, he carefully took his position on the horizontal platform in order to dredge the oyster bed. The long, slim handles of the tongs were big and clumsy and weighed heavily, swaying to and fro as Ebb attempted to maneuver the vise. It was not until Bo helped that Ebb was able to slide the steel teeth into the hole and work them back and forth against the uneven mound below. When the load got heavy, they struggled to retrieve the salty catch, pulling and slipping and finally bringing the long burdensome handles down and about, towing the heavily laden cage over the ice and to a spot well-removed from the stand. When they had sorted their spoils, five big crusty bluepoint oysters lay glistening on the ice. Ebb and Bo happily set the mollusks neatly side by side and with their penknives attempted to shuck their catch. The oysters stubbornly resisted. It was only when the boys smashed the jagged edges of the shells and forced the narrow blades into the oysters' muscles, cranking the instruments back and forth and severing their tendons, that the fight was gone, and the shells opened easily and were ready to eat. The oysters sat shimmering gray and green and eggy in the cold winter sunlight. Ebb and Bo looked uncertainly at them.

"It didn't look too good," Ebb admitted and chuckled with reminiscent delight as he recalled the episode:

Bo hadn't ever seen an oyster close up. I told 'em that since it was his first time seein' an oyster, the first one was his to eat. But he insisted that he didn't know how and had to learn.

"You the expert," Bo said. "You ain't ate the first one till somebody teach you!"

86

"Yeah, but lookit," I insisted. "You see that?"
I pointed to the oyster with my knife. "That's the
best there is. . . ."—and I weren't lying then. For
sure that oyster looked better than any oyster I
seen that day. The shell was blistered some, but
not blistered so bad and muddy as the others. Talk
as I did, there was no puttin' anything over on Bo.
Hesitantly, I held the oyster careful high, said my
secret prayer and gobbled down that oyster as fast
as I could.

"What ya holdin' ya breath for?" Bo asked. I
thought I'd die and hung my head down and slowly
'came relieved.

"You sure missed somethin'!" I wiped my
mouth and picked up the other oyster.
"Ummmmmmmm-MMMMMM! They sure is
good," I insisted, and made like I was gonna eat
the second one. You shoulda seen 'em.

"You don't want this one, do you?" I asked.

"No!" he said certain, and waited for me to
swallow that second oyster.

Bo never before said "no" to somethin' I done
first and that surprised me. But I weren't 'bout to
eat another oyster.

"We're blood brothers, ain't we?" I said.

Bo, as uncertain as he was on oysters, knowed
that blood brothers gotta do what blood brothers
do, even if they die eatin' oysters. After looking
north and looking south three times, he knowed
what he got to do. He held the old barnacled shell
to the tip of his bottom lip. His eyes was big as
saucers and stared cross-eyed at the slimy critter.

"Now!" I yelled.

Bo blinked his eyes, closed his mouth and swallowed hard. "Bo, you all right?" I asked, fearing
for his health.

Bo wabbled his mouth enough to say, " 'Sit gone?"

He woulda stood there forever as a monument to oyster eatin' if I hadn't said, "You done it!" He was mad and didn't say nothin' for a spell till I asked 'em if he wanted another.

"What you say that for?" he asked.

"Say what?"

" 'Now'—and 'swallow it' and all! You don't hafta tell me!"

I ain't ever seen Bo madder and told 'em that I was sorry and wouldn't say nothin' again like that. Bo said he weren't for eatin' oysters anymore and was gonna put his oysters back to bed 'cus he felt sorry for such even though they tasted good. I agreed, and that's what we done.

CHAPTER 14

THERE was an unearthly hush as old life waited expectantly in the dusk of day. Amongst the coastal pines, the somber trickle of a feeder stream wound its way to a tidal pool. The forest came to rest as the languid fog settled in the warmth of the night. It was early April, only days beyond the vernal equinox. Deep shadows no longer bowed to the winter's sun, for the mighty star Regulus now reigned high. At 7:47 p.m. the last vestige of daylight escaped into the night; the ritual and splendor of creation unfolded in the brackish waters of a sequestered pool. A great striped bass broke the silence with the clap of life, dancing and jostling in the ecstatic struggle and lust for procreation. This anadromous fish rolled freely as did others in the light of the new crested moon. Eggs, green as the eyes of Anubis, burst forth as translucent pearls and were scattered to the currents of time. In these waters replete with milt, the eggs drifted for weeks, some for months, suspended in the tides. One fertilized egg which did not sink or bob, but rode the upper touches of the drift, survived and remained the one in 100,000 to live. In six weeks this small-fry would join the other survivors and school. For them, the hunt would begin.

Contentedly, the parent fish rode the river currents back to the sea and the rich Chesapeake estuary.

Spring lapsed into summer and all things were done in harmony until July of that year. It was then that the incident occurred which spared none the comforts of illusion and will be forgotten by few.

Prince Frederick is the largest municipality in Calvert County and the closest town to Solomons Island by fifteen miles. It has taken on the appearance of time, although the structures are relatively new compared to most in the county. In 1890, an electric storm burned the town to the ground. Then in 1933, along came a Georgia gentleman by the name of "Singing Sam," originally an Irish immigrant from the county Antrim, Ireland, and of the noble clan of O'Donnellan.

"Smarter than a whip with words he was. But he drank!" reflected Mr. Poe. "Matter-a-fact he drank it up so much one day that he came out of the local saloon walkin' like a cross-eyed rooster hollerin' 'Yellar.' Next day, Prince Frederick was burnt down 'gain. Two people was killed and Singing Sam was burnt bad. 'Fore he died, he told them people that he just didn't like the color yellar, the color of the saloon, mind ya."

The people of Solomons Island refer to Prince Frederick as the "burnt-out town" and insist that the town never grew back, just got uglier and nastier—akin to chimaeras, only more strange in its subtle way. Such remarks can be attributed to the fact that Prince Frederick has been the county seat for seventy years. Feuding ensued, the likes of which enlivened the language considerably and excited the adrenalin to the point of perverse antipathy, leading Solomons people to consider Prince Frederick people rather snooty and unneighborly. Luckily, Prince Frederick has an event each year that dissolves emotional qualms and any hard feelings that may exist between the communal factions. That occasion is the arrival of the Barnum and Bailey Circus.

According to Ebb, William Bodecker had never seen a circus and, as Ebb explained, the anticipation exhibited by Bo was exhilarating and added a new and refreshing dimension to the event.

As was the custom, each Saturday morning of the summer months was reserved for Ebb to travel with his uncle into Prince Frederick to sell his harvest of softshell crabs. It was on such an occasion that Ebb saw circus men pasting a big, colorful poster of "The Greatest Show on Earth" on the old Creekhouse barn right beneath the perennial exhibit of "Mail Pouch Chewing Tobacco." The notice led Ebb to persuade his uncle that selling crabs on such a hot day "done spoiled the crabs unmercifully" and that he himself suffered from a fatigue caused by a "Prince Frederick sunstroke." In due course they hurried home, only to have Ebb recover from his malady as soon as they reached the outskirts of Solomons Island. Ebb feigned that he had suddenly remembered a chore of utter necessity and disappeared in the direction of Custus' pine wood, the shortest route to Shanty, Bo's home.

Now, as Ebb had learned previously, Shanty was reputed to be off limits to white folk and, according to protocol, was the place where "the surest trouble was waitin' if you as much sneezed past its bounds." However, Bo prescribed to Ebb that the best and safest way was to approach Shanty by the outhouse.

"Dat's where the spirits live," Bo said earnestly. "Nobody fools with them spirits near dat place, not even Shanty people. If the spirits does bothers you, you go—ERKE . . . ERKE . . . ERKE . . . rrrrreeeee-eeeeee! You know, like a chicken. Spirits likes the chicken."

91

The outhouse sat inconspicuously on the edge of the pine wood, a half-mile south of the main thoroughfare and approximately four hundred feet from the river. Two short, bushy pine trees hid its entrance. Ebb cautiously snuck up past it to the trees, and was about to separate the branches to scout what was beyond, when he heard a scolding voice, more instructive than angry, echo from the recesses of Bo's house. A door opened. Ebb peeked around a pine bough just in time to see Bo tramp down the porch stairs. His lower lip was rolled in contempt. He jumped from the last three stairs, stumbling as he landed, but miraculously checking his fall with the large stick he was carrying. His ma immediately followed, carrying a rug which she attached to a clothesline.

"Now you beat that rug till you get out every inch a dust. I don't want you talkin' all day either. You hear me?" She spoke firmly, shaking her finger unflaggingly at Bo and walked hurriedly back to the house. As she opened the screen door, she stopped momentarily and looked back at Bo, shook her head disapprovingly, then quietly closed the screen door behind her. Bo wasted little time in venting his displeasure. He jumped and shouted obscenities and commenced to circle the rug with a vengeance and determination befitting David and Goliath, hitting it with unabridged fury, only to have his ma reappear.

"William Bodecker!!!"

Such surveillance brought a rash of faces the likes of which Ebb had never seen. The threat of another confrontation with his ma calmed Bo considerably. He commenced to beat the rug slowly and with little fanfare.

Ebb hesitantly called, "Bo! Psssssssst. Bo!" Bo perked his ears.

"Psssssssst! Hey, Bo!"

Bo stopped his work. Caught unveiled in temper, he resented Ebb's discovery and turned his head in Ebb's direction, pretending uncertainty as to the voice, and said contemptuously, "Who is it?"

"It's me, Ebb."

Just as Bo was about to open his mouth, Ebb saw Bo's mother sneak a look out of the window. "Hit the rug! Hit the rug!" Ebb said in a frenzy.

Still unraveled by the series of events which had beset him, Bo retorted, "What you mean, 'hit the rug'?" Bo turned quizzically toward Ebb and, with sarcastic flair, said matter-of-factly, "What you think I's doin'?"

"You ma!" Ebb jumped back behind the tree.

Bo, clever at handling impromptu circumstances, widened his eyes and waved that big stick high in the air, turned in a complete circle, and "let out one of the fieriest rug-beatin' yells" anyone has ever heard. The sound rang through the woods and you would have thought that rug had blown apart. Dust flew in all directions. Bo's ma stuck her head further out of the window.

"Now is that the way I taught you to thrash a rug?" she inquired. She stared at Bo long enough to make him uneasy and then continued her plaint. "You better simmer down child or you . . . is gonna be . . . on the opposite end OF THAT STICK—YOU HEAR ME?"

She continued her watch until she was satisfied with Bo's improved behavior, then quickly disappeared again into the darkness of the house. Ebb, frightened at his tenuous position and vexed with his indecision as to stay or retreat, was relieved to hear Bo's casual reaction.

"Ebb—you still there?"

"Yeah!"

"What ya got up?"

Ebb, sensing the electricity of the moment, mouthed the words in appropriate order before repeating them to Bo. He had long decided that however demure his address Bo's response would be fervent if not fanatical, and so, taking a deep breath, he whispered loud enough to be heard over Bo's rhythmic rug beat, "Bo, the circus comin' to town."

Bo continued to swat the rug with persistent vigor, as he digested the full content of the message.

"The circus poster is at the old barn in Prince Frederick," Ebb continued. "It's gonna be here in one week. There's this big elephant called 'Jumbo.' You'll see it—the biggest ever!"

Bo, by this time, looked as if he were sunstruck. Ebb, however, in his zeal, spoke on enthusiastically, leaving Bo to romanticize visions of fantasy and the world of the circus. The rug never got done.

CHAPTER **15**

EBB, in his omniscient tall-tale version of circus lore, expressed a thorough, steadfast formulation for "studying and figuring the circus."

"You gotta spend lots of years and hard work knowing who does what, where this and that goes and all."

The next day, Bo and Ebb hitched a ride to Prince Frederick and surveyed the circus site. Circus riggers had already prepared the grounds and had measured the appropriate emplacements for tents and animals.

"See that markin', Bo?" Ebb pointed enthusiastically to the red marker bearing a white slip of cloth. "That's where they gonna put the most fiercest lion. See the red. Over here's where . . ." Bo, at times, assumed an expression of utter disbelief, all the while scratching his head and staring seriously and observantly at the ground and across the field.

"God! You see what I see? They musta marked out room for a million elephants."

Bo gaped at the same spot. "Yeaaaaaaaah—I see it. Ain't that somethin'!" he lied. He occasionally dramatized his credence with attentive flashes of awe.

On the day before the circus was to arrive in Prince Frederick, Ebb informed Bo of the importance of keeping a diligent vigil out for the arrival of the circus train. That night, they sat together in the middle of the field (designated as the Big Top sanctuary by Ebb) and waited in silent expectation for "The Greatest Show on Earth."

The night was warm and clear and peaceful. The rhythmic cadence of crickets enfolded the darkness in nocturnal ritual. Many wondrous shadows moved sleekly in the bright moonlight, rendering visions of disproportionment and freakish apparitions. Distant voices, clear and constant, wore on into the balmy night, the soothing drone of which brought Ebb and Bo to lie heavily on the warm, dry hay. Casually, they chewed grass weeds and gazed contentedly at the stars.

Bo took the first watch. He searched the darkness like a true scout. Bent forward in anticipation, his every sense was alert. Occasionally, Ebb heard Bo sniff the air deeply. It made Ebb proud of Bo because, as Ebb explained, "That's what ya have to do if ya gonna do it right."

After the night had fully set in, the usual precautions were forgotten and casual chat followed at a normal pace until Bo finally said nothing more. Ebb later recalled that it was almost at that moment of complete silence when he faintly heard a familiar sound, foreign in time, but unmistakably clear to his thought. He shook his head to revive his senses, but the unwonted stupor made him think his euphoric impression was a dream.

Bo was sound asleep. The night was darker than Ebb had ever remembered. He suspected that he, too, had fallen asleep. But the sound persisted.

"Click, click, click."

Ebb shook Bo excitedly and stood up to affirm his suspicions.

A heaviness moved stealthily in the darkness, its effect even and slow and long until it screeched small in the night and came to a silence. Bo and Ebb strained their eyes in the hush of blackness. There was a presence, imminent and fissiparous. Suddenly, a small, white light appeared in the distance, accentuating the night, its orb expanding and diminishing with each movement to and fro.

"C'mon, Bo!" cried Ebb. Excitedly, the two of them ran, stumbling across the field. As they approached the light, it shone brighter and bigger. In awe, they stopped and stared at the mightiest train they had ever seen. Ebb described it as "a giant, black snake, long and streamlined." The engine was motionless. Steam seeped steadily from beneath its enormous carriage.

"Dem lions and gorillas ain't come charging out of dat, does they?" Bo asked apprehensively.

"I don't think so," said Ebb. Quietly, they inched backward, all the while keeping a suspicious eye on the trail of box cars extending far into the darkness.

Without warning, a large incandescent light exploded the darkness into the brightness of day. Big, ghostly shadows stood up out of the night. The heavy, wooden gates of the circus cars slowly creaked downward. And a storybook opened up before their eyes. People of all sizes and shapes came dancing and walking and jumping from the train. Some had dogs or carried monkeys or led camels. Others pulled ropes and pushed carts and carried some of the funniest, prettiest things that Bo and Ebb had ever seen. Then came the elephants, big like the train itself, ambling slowly and heavily down the planks. Once they reached the ground, they picked up speed as if they were happy where they were, and even happier where they were going.

As Ebb recalled, "Jungle boys quick walked 'em, hitched 'em up to wide harnesses and backed 'em up to the big train again. Ropes, bigger than a man's arm, were hooked to the harness. At a signal, the big gray elephants, like they knowed exactly what they were up to, pulled hard and steady, and out rolled the Big Top. More and more elephants came until it seemed like there was tons of 'em snorting and blowing air. Those that didn't work stood in a straight line like they'd come for inspection. Circus men locked big, iron chains around their hind legs and secured 'em to deep-set spikes. Some elephants had two chains. But one elephant got three. He was the biggest and fiercest, you could tell. For sure that was Jumbo, and we stood and watched him especially. When he swayed, the earth moved and he blocked out the sky from front of us."

His beady red eyes had nearly hypnotized Ebb, when Ebb suddenly realized that he and Bo hadn't moved too far from where they had originally sighted the train. Dawn was breaking on the horizon, soft and blue. Ebb turned to Bo. "Hey, Bo! What we standin' here all the time for?"

Bo, absorbed with the flood of activity, acknowledged Ebb's question with only the slightest nod of his head and murmured, "Yeah!" According to Ebb, that was the most Bo said for most of that day.

"C'mon, Bo. We gotta see if they need help with the elephants."

Circus people are reputed to be among the most efficient and fast-working people in the world. As Ebb explained, they paint pictures before your eyes. They laid the Big Top out on the ground within its designated perimeter. Ropes strained and elephants pulled. The men hollered and cussed. Big, steel rings were slowly hoisted up the center pole and the tent, as if it breathed, came alive with air. Work crews joined together in propping up the side poles, making the tent taut and secure to the ground. Ebb and Bo stood their distance and watched with fascination as the work went on. A big, burly man, ruddy in complexion and quick of tongue, pointed them out to one of the crew. More confused than surprised, Ebb and Bo walked into each other and then continued to walk in their opposite directions.

"Hey, you men!"

Ebb and Bo looked around simultaneously to see who had addressed them.

"You . . ." The man pointed to the boys, nodding his head approvingly and waving his large, fat hand for them to approach him. ". . . you workin' men?" he asked them.

"Ya . . . ye . . . yes, sir," Ebb's words faded out in uncertainty.

"Well then, jump in here and earn your meal!" The circus man looked as serious a man as Bo and Ebb had ever seen, and with due respect they quickly grabbed a rope. Eight men, counting Bo and Ebb, pulled while a black man sang. Then they all started in: "Heave . . . ho, ho. Heave . . . ho, ho. Heave . . ."

The rope was big and hard and raw in the boys' young hands. When they heaved, the rope carried a mighty weight. Bo flew off the ground on the first "ho," but pride kept him firm the next time and he spent many a strenuous moment on his tiptoes. The men didn't say much, but Ebb observed, "You could tell they liked what they was doin'." According to Ebb, they put up nearly a million poles before a whistle, shrill as a train whistle, pierced the morning air. It was circus lunch time—10 a.m. The circus boss stood nearby and casually passed out stubby yellow tickets bearing the number "3." He gave one each to Bo and Ebb, but as they turned to follow the other workers to the food tent, the circus foreman called them back.

99

He reached gingerly into his shirt pocket and pulled out two shiny, red tickets.

"You boys did a fine job," the foreman said gratefully and handed the tickets to Ebb and Bo. Bemused by their good fortune, they dared not look at their bonus. At their politest best they said in unison, "Thank ya, sir!"

Such sweet talk filled Ebb with laughter inside and although his tact was impeccable, the circus man intuitively understood the intonation and his seriousness cracked with a smile. "I thought right then, he weren't so mean as he put on," Ebb said later.

A stubby yellow ticket got a ham sandwich with a slip of lettuce on white bread spiced with mustard, a pint carton of white milk and a small piece of deep, yellow pound cake. Ebb and Bo agreed it was the tastiest meal they both had ever experienced away from home. The circus people came and went in quick succession. Everyone sat together at long tables placed temporarily beneath a white tent. They ate noisily. Bo and Ebb had set their bright red tickets up against the milk cartons where they could examine them thoroughly and, most important, keep them under close surveillance. Ebb curiously looked at Bo's ticket and Bo likewise looked at Ebb's:

WORK PASS

ADMIT ONE

BARNUM AND BAILEY CIRCUS

They both had smiles bigger than Cheshire cats.

Their good fortune completely changed their eating habits. They wolfed their food with a gusto not for taste, but for the expectation of all that lay before them. It was at that moment when Bo was about to drink down the last mouthful of milk that a dwarf, "a real live one," came up and sat down by Bo. According to Ebb, "Bo near stopped breathing and didn't move a bone.

The dwarf ate fast, faster than you'd suspect a dwarf to eat—and after he finished he sat smokin' a cigarette."

"What's he doin'?" Ebb whispered to Bo.

Bo poked Ebb with his elbow. Captivated by the event, Bo stared wonderingly ahead, silent and unapproachable.

"We musta waited a million years," Ebb related, "until that dwarf finally got up and walked out the tent. When Bo came back to life and finished his milk, I knowed what he was gonna say, so I didn't ask 'em. But he told me anyway, and it come out all day on how the dwarf touched him and all."

The circus grounds got busier as the day wore on. Barkers progressively voiced their wares until the culmination of activity bloomed into full circus reveille, rendering the atmosphere devoid of singularity and pleasing the mind with a multitude of colors and exotica. It was a land transformed into tons of popcorn and acres of sawdust. Bright, cheery flags flew from every pole, and clowns, mimicking the faces of joy, stood at every corner. Circus stands were festooned with balloons, Kewpie dolls and an endless array of other small toys. Ebb felt an immediate urge to join the circus. When he turned to tell Bo about his thought, he gasped to see that Bo didn't have his ticket in his hand. In desperation, Ebb grabbed Bo's arm.

"Where's you ticket, Bo?" Ebb asked excitedly.

Bo pointed to his shoe and grinned.

"Honest!" Ebb said incredulously.

"Honest! Dat's where I got it." Bo sat down on the ground and pulled off his big, dusty brown shoe. He carefully looked about to assure himself that nobody was looking and carefully rolled off his sock. Confidently he held up his foot for Ebb to see and sure enough there was that ticket glued to the bottom of his foot. Ebb told Bo that it was one of the smartest ideas he had ever witnessed, and to show his good faith, Ebb took off his shoe and did the same. Ebb's decision made Bo prouder than a peacock, but as Ebb admitted, "Walking thereafter was most difficult and not much for want. You might of thought we was cripples for the rest of the circus."

CHAPTER 16

OW keeping that circus ticket was a question of deep concern. "Keep it forever. Yessuh!" Bo would say. Ebb couldn't blame him for his frugality, since the tickets were good for one show *only* and that show, Ebb stressed, "might be the last show we see forever." However, little time passed before a solution presented itself. Out of the darkness Ebb and Bo spotted three boys moving with stealthy intent, then right before their eyes the boys scooted under the heavy canvas of the Big Top. "They got in 'cus they ain't come out." Ebb looked at Bo in amazement.

"You don't think they's killed, do ya?" Bo asked seriously.

"Naaaa, you don't get killed in the circus. That's why they call it the circus!" Ebb reassured Bo of the amenities of circus life and with a flamboyant display of confidence added, "All you gotta do is shake you shoe for good luck."

In like manner, Bo and Ebb stood by the chosen spot and leaned casually against a taut mooring rope. Guilt amplified their watch as horses stomped heavily off into the bright lights. Clowns, dwarfs and—as Ebb explained—even a witch, with "wobbly snakes in her hair," stared amusedly at Ebb and Bo, and wickedly smiled. Such insidious behavior imbued in Ebb an impression of the ultimate curse. He urgently called to Bo, "C'mon, Bo!" And with a "better-than-not" attitude, they escaped to the tent wall and rolled quickly under the weighty canvas. A large, red wagon hid them from view. The air hung heavy with exotic odors. They cautiously peered around the big, spoked wheel of the wagon to stare directly into a glaring light. Silhouetted against the monstrous orb, the dark shadow of a man came forth quickly until his huge bulk was upon them.

"Get away from there!" he hollered. "Get away!" Dumbfounded by their discovery, Ebb and Bo crouched fearfully behind the wheel and grabbed the smooth, wooden spokes determinedly.

"Go on! You know you're not supposed to be here!" The man grabbed Ebb and Bo each by the arm and rushed them off to a roped-in section of the tent where people had gathered and were watching.

"You want to get killed?" the circus attendant asked sternly.

"No, sir!" they answered and, confused, looked quizzically back toward the red circus wagon. Sitting in a cage on top of the wagon was a huge gorilla. It stared bleakly, silently out at the crowd. An engraved, wooden panel atop the cage read:

GARGANTUA
The Biggest Gorilla in Captivity

It had been a good day for Ebb and Bo. They were full of cotton candy and watermelon, peanuts and ice cream. By the time night set in, they had seen as much as they had hoped to see for one day. They lay high on the side of the cook tent and relaxed in the deep shadows. The canvas was warm from the day's sun. The smell of cooked food wafted amongst the tents. Ebb's eyelids became heavy as a pleasant, wondrous fatigue enveloped his body. He had almost fallen asleep when Bo said, "Ebb, you ever seen a goo?"

Ebb, lost in lethargy, and unsure of what the word "goo" meant, shook his head and replied hesitantly, "What you mean, a 'goo'?"

"I seen this sign, THE GOO. You see it?"

"Yeah, I seen it," Ebb professed quickly. He turned away to assume a more somnolent posture, but was soon interrupted again by Bo's insistent chatter.

"I never seen a goo. You?" Bo continued.

"Yeah."

"Well, ain't you wanta see this one?" Bo asked insistently.

It was unusual for Ebb to get provoked, but as Ebb related, the constant interruption of his pleasant reveries surely raised his temper and led him to let loose with what he referred to as "the devil's tongue." He sat up angrily and said, "Why, ain't you ever seen people ate?"

Bo turned abruptly toward Ebb and excitedly inquired, "People ate! What you mean, 'people ate'?"

"Cannibals do it," Ebb said confidently.

"Yeah, but the goo ain't no cannibal."

"Yeah, he is. He's the worst kind. A real cannibal give you a chance. The goo, he don't give you no chance!" While Ebb relaxed on the subject, Bo pondered cannibalism versus goo-ism.

Bo, annoyed by so profound an implication, asked "What you mean, he don't give you no chance?"

"Just what I said, he don't give you a chance."

"That sure don't sound like a goo to me," Bo said, unconvinced.

Ebb, prompted to assuage Bo's fears, said, "You don't have to worry none, Bo. This goo's my friend. He gives you a chance. He's the onliest goo I know who will."

Bo listened intently. Caught in the fantasy of his story and inspired by Bo's preoccupation with ghouls, Ebb willingly continued. "You probably thinking about what the goo looks like, ain't ya, Bo? . . . Remember that gorilla we seen, hairy and big and mean? Well, the goo's like him. Only the goo's got a tooth longer than any you ever seen. Even bigger than the gorilla's got. It stick out of his mouth right here in front. He got arms and legs long and powerful with the biggest, sharpest claws you ever seen. He don't pay ya no heed, either. He just kill ya right off. Even eat you, too, if he want."

Ebb lay contentedly back on the tent again, proud that he could think of such a story. "*Arabian Nights* couldn't a been better," he thought to himself. A fanfare of music from a calliope started somewhere in the distance. A lion roared lazily. Ebb's eyes focused on a horizon full of tents and slowly began to close, when Bo said, "You ain't no friend of no goo 'cus he ain't ever been here 'fore!"

Ebb, convinced that the night would be long, bounced up with authority and looked straight into Bo's eyes. "Bo, how long you been in the club?"

Bo hesitated and shook his head uncertainly. "A year?"

"A year! You out of your mind! How long you known me?"

"Near a year and some."

"And you don't know me past that, ain't that right?"

Bo, feigning deafness, said nothing. Ebb jumped down off the tent, turned to face Bo and said emphatically, "I been in the club ever since I've been here, and that's since I can remember!" He turned abruptly around and walked toward the ferris wheel in the distance. Ebb was sorry that he had treated Bo as harshly

106

as he had, but he was determined not to show any sympathy. He hadn't walked three steps before he heard Bo jump down from the tent and start to follow.

By the tenth step Bo said in a smug, challenging voice, "If you his friend, why don't you go see 'em?"

Ebb stopped in his tracks and looked glaringly back at Bo. He remained silent and commenced to walk again. This time, however, he was walking in the direction of the ghoul's tent.

"Where you goin'?" Bo insisted.

"Ta see the goo." Ebb's gait became noticeably more determined.

"Ta see the goo!" Bo cried out. He stopped where he was and sat stubbornly down on the ground.

Ebb walked calmly on until he was sure Bo wasn't following. He turned and yelled back with flippant relief, "Bo, you comin' or not?"

"No! I ain't goin' see no goo!"

"Why not? You scared?"

"I ain't scared. He's *you* friend, not mine."

"You's scared, I know."

Ebb, thinking the situation was well in hand, checked to measure visually his safe distance from the ghoul's tent. Suddenly, Bo jumped up and hurried toward him.

"I ain't scared, dat's what I know! You ain't scared 'cus you got a knife with ya. Who's gonna be scared if you got dat?"

Ebb stood dumbfounded.

"Bo, you is stupid! S . . . T . . . U . . . P . . . I . . . E . . . D. You want the knife?"

Perturbed, Ebb reached into his pants pocket and pulled out his penknife. He held it out on the palm of his hand.

Without hesitation, Bo walked quickly over to Ebb and took the penknife. Victoriously, Bo put it safely into his pocket. They both walked cautiously in the direction of the fairway until they came to the sign:

THE GHOUL
SEE IT TO BELIEVE IT
Most Savage Creature in Captivity
Eats Animals Alive
NEXT MEAL—10:30

"You gotta give the knife back if I need it, Bo, you hear?" Ebb looked at Bo for assurance. Bo had his hand in his pocket. A wry smile brushed his face.

A hunchbacked man, his skin withered by sun and age, stood at the opening to the tent. Ebb and Bo, suspecting that this man might well be the ghoul himself, tried to ignore his presence. They would have walked right past him had they not been grabbed brusquely by their collars. They froze in their tracks, not daring to look back.

"Where's your money, boys?" the man asked calmly.

Ebb quickly pulled out a dime from his pocket and gave it to the waiting attendant.

"Bo, give 'em you money."

Bo frantically searched in his shirt pocket, pulled out another dime, and handed it to the man. The heinous character shook his ugly head. "That's not enough boys," he said. "Two more dimes."

"That's all the money we got," Ebb said sadly.

The ugly man said nothing. Despondently, Ebb and Bo turned to leave, allowing the man to keep what they had given him out of respectful fear, when unexpectedly he said, "OK—go on in!" and pushed them quickly into the tent.

108

CHAPTER 17

EBB recalled that the tent in which the ghoul event took place was curiously small. People had to stoop to enter the cramped area. The air was foul and the audience sweated profusely. The closeness made breathing difficult. The dimly lit space became a cage in itself; there was no room to move about unless, as Ebb explained, one took up residence with the ghoul himself. Visions raced through Ebb's mind of the ghoul escaping from his cage and choosing him for the feast. In the middle of the tent, a small incandescent white light shone coldly over a roped section containing a small square cage, its top and sides hidden beneath a green-stained tarp. Crudely painted signs hung conspicuously on each side of the cage:

PLEASE DON'T FEED THE GHOUL

Occasionally, the cage would shake furiously under its cover, its weary inhabitant emitting strange and foreign noises, the likes of which raised hairs and goose pimples and conjured up visions of the most unworldly aberration. A small boy cried hysterically. His mother picked him up and told him that "it ain't for real" and that he would "see." From out of the crowd, a man stepped into the forbidden and foreboding circle. It was the same man who had given Ebb and Bo their first circus tickets! He wore a powder-blue satin shirt adorned with silver sequins and dark blue jodhpurs. A large silver belt buckle bespoke Herculean authority. He carried a short bullwhip in his right hand and a live chicken in the other. With hawk-like quickness he unfurled the whip.

"Ladies and gentlemen!" he addressed the audience as he held the chicken high. All gazed in wonder.

". . . Ladies and gentlemen! Tonight, you will witness, in this very cage, the beast of death itself. The ghoul!"

The circus man cracked the whip. Its leather thongs slapped loudly against the awning. Then he warned the audience, "If anyone . . . any one of you in this audience cannot bear to witness . . . death! . . . please leave this tent now, before it is too late!"

No one moved. Nor could they move. A slight rustle was heard from inside the cage. The circus man slowly untied the front side of the tarp and then quickly yanked its covering back. The chicken, frightened by the sudden movement, flapped its wings and squawked loudly. The cage was dark and forbidding. Two red, evil eyes peered out from within. A big, black, powerful arm suddenly shot out from the cage, catching the chicken by the tail feathers. The whip, as though alive, quickly snapped around the ghoul's arm. The ghoul let loose a cry of sincere pain and anger and fled back into the shadows of the cage.

"Men died trying to capture this beast. Four men! Four!" the circus man repeated, holding up four fingers. He milled about searching the faces in the crowd. The effect he had had pleased him. He continued his story. "The great Frank Buck hunted for this creature

110

for many years without success. Legend has it that a great ghoul guarded over the tomb of Inga, the stone god of Borneo. All the great explorers of the world went in search of his tomb and a great stone which marked his presence."

His voice dropped as he continued, "In this tomb there was a stone of many powers. A sacred red stone. The stone of death. The ghoul stone!"

From out of the darkness, the hunchbacked man appeared. He was holding a reddish stone. He held it high with spontaneous delight. A small spotlight drifted above the raised heads and came to rest on the stone. The ghoul-man howled like a wolf.

"Take a good look, ladies and gentlemen!" The circus man pointed to the shining omen. "There is only one stone of its kind in existence," he told them. "The story behind it will make you shudder. The powers of this night are as wicked as the powers of *that* evil night —the night we first discovered the ghoul!"

There followed a silence. A formidable silence. The audience stirred in anticipation. The circus man continued, "A man died mysteriously at the first archaeological site we surveyed in Borneo. The earth there was strangely ashen. The trees were gray and bent tortuously earthward. A hole which we discovered, two feet in circumference, was smoldering and emitting sulphuric vapors. The smell of death hung in the air. The sun was hidden by its yellowish veil. We buried the man quickly. You may ask the question, why? Well, for good reason! That man began to take on the appearance of the creature you see before you!"

The spectators nearest the cage moved slightly back from the circle. The circus man, heartened by the response, became even more intense in his presentation.

"We spent the night keeping fires lit to keep this evil away from our camp. As a full moon moved to its ze-

111

nith, silence fell around us. Slowly, very slowly, the blood-curdling cry of the ancient ghoul rose steadily in the tropical night. We were terrified. We asked ourselves, who would be the next victim?

"The next morning, the red stone of death shone brightly from the grave. I knew that the tale of the sacred ghoul was true. My men threw nets over the grave and prodded the ground until the earth moved violently. A deep, gurgling voice came from the mound and this ghoul . . . this very ghoul you see here tonight . . . raised his blood-soaked face from the ominous pit. He bit through the thickest rope. He attacked and mutilated three of my men before we could secure a steel net around him."

The circus man raised his voice with resolve. "Sad as I am to say," he continued, "all three men, all of them, died from the ghoul's venomous bite. Ladies and gentlemen—this is a killer!"

As if on cue, the circus ghoul wildly shook his cage. Violently, he bent an "iron" bar prepared for the prank. People pointed, but the circus man had intentionally turned his back. "This same ghoul," he continued, "tasted human blood two months ago in Dallas, Texas. He caught a young man and tore his head right from his shoulders. Please—PLEASE be careful where you stand."

At that warning, the people pressed back toward the entrance. One middle-aged lady fainted. Her husband yanked her up and with an awkward, insensitive sweep of his hand slapped her face sharply and said, "C'mon, honey, you don't wanta miss this. C'mon!"

Those who were shoved back now pushed forward until the people in front were shoved slowly toward the cage. Many became scared and began shouting obscenities. Suddenly, the ghoul grabbed the chicken by the neck and forced the bird between the bars. Feath-

112

ers flew in all directions. Blood squirted inside the cage. The ghoul howled again. Its terrifying cry sent shivers of fear throughout the crowd. Suddenly, the lights went out. People screamed. Then the small spotlight appeared again. Its beam floated over and around the crowd and came finally to the cage of the ghoul. In the shadows, defiant eyes stared pitiously into the void, not seeing the crowd, but blinded in despair and shame. The ghoul's teeth were blood-stained. He guarded his catch jealously. Ebb let his eyes drop down to the ghoul's thighs. He was surprised to see that the creature wore pants. He turned to tell Bo, only to find Bo occupied with keeping his thumbs in his ears and his fingers over his eyes.

"Bo, you all right?"

Startled, Bo glanced at Ebb and mumbled some words between his fingers. As he did so, the main lights came on again. Ebb quickly looked around and saw a drop of the chicken's blood on Bo's T-shirt. A sure premonition, he thought.

The circus man pulled the heavy tarpaulin back over the cage. A hand reached up from the crowd and grabbed a feather that was floating aimlessly about the tent. The odor of vomit was now heavy in the close air. Ebb looked at Bo's shirt again, and the wet, thick crimson blood. He was tempted to warn Bo, but hesitated on seeing the hunchbacked man standing at the square directing the movement of the dazed crowd. Ebb and Bo moved slowly toward the exit and finally, with a sigh of relief, came out into the abundant fresh air. Ebb said that it picked his lungs up and made him glad that the world "ain't a tent." As they exited, Bo stepped to the side and turned quizzically toward Ebb.

In a concerned yet confused voice, Bo asked, "Is all de goos black?"

"What ya mean—black?" As Ebb spoke, a sudden,

steady breeze blew silently in from the east. Massive black clouds followed, shutting out the stars as they swept across the night sky. Thunder broke the heavens with shattering reverberation, as the lightning transformed the circus tents into cabalistic images of mythical giants. The rain came as suddenly as the wind had. Big, heavy droplets splayed and wafted the powdery dust of the circus grounds. People scurried to the Big Top. As the deluge of rain began, Ebb and Bo darted back into the ghoul's tent. They slid down behind the ticket stand and sat silently. The lights in the tent flickered and slowly went out. Rhythmically, the tent flashed white to the thunderous cadence in the sky. The earth trembled. As Ebb described it:

Suddenly, a big lightning bolt struck the earth. I coulda sworn the tent was gonna crash down. Its sides heaved in and out like a giant bellows. Another lightning bolt shot through the circus like it come to stay. The devils of that night was awakened from their sleep for sure. Strange, frightened cries filled the tent that night. Bo and me looked around, scared as anything. In the lightning white of the storm we saw the tarpaulin of the ghoul's cage move. And in the next light there stood that ghoul himself, black and ugly, hunched over and near unable to stand—howling in the stormy night.

Bo and me fell flat to the ground, scared like never before. Then we heard a voice what relieved us something big. It was the voice of the circus man. We looked up and saw him standing over the ghoul. He unfurled his big whip. The ghoul, like he knowed what was coming, covered his head with his arms. That whip came down hard more than once, each time making that ghoul wail in pain.

"You son-of-a-bitch," the circus man cried

114

aloud. ". . . all I've done for you. You black son-of-a-bitch!" His whip lashed out again till the ghoul fell to his knees.

"It's too many times you've done this, boy. Too many! I'm takin' you to the sheriff. That's what you want?"

The ghoul whimpered and held his head down. The circus man got mad again—even angrier, and impatiently said, "Speak to me, nigger! Is that what you want?"

The circus boss put his big shoe on the ghoul's shoulder and shoved him hard as he could. The ghoul rolled over, and like a craw worm, he came undone and lay flat on the ground. Thunder rattled off in the distance and the rain fell light. The lights came on. And then, like we don't believe our ears, that ghoul spoke. He said, "No, sir. I's a sick man, Mr. Gress. I's awful sick."

"You're not kidding me, mister," the circus man sneered. "Your head's sick. That's what's wrong. All you want is something for nothing."

The circus man thought for a moment and said, "You know, you're the most spiteful nigger I've ever known. Now, you get back in that cage! You don't get out again unless you're told. You hear me, nigger!"

"No, Mr. Gress! No!" the ghoul begged feebly. "I beg ya. You can't do dat."

The circus boss stood over the ghoul, looking down with meanness and hate in his twisted smile. He pointed to the cage. "IN!" he commanded. He began to unfurl his whip again, but that ghoul, he didn't want no more beatin'. He crawled slow 'cross the sawdust to the cage and disappeared under the canopy—only this time, we heard a lock snap shut.

Then I heard the ghoul again, crying and saying,

"You can't do dat to me. You can't do dat, Mr. Gress."

The hunchbacked ticket-taker walked from out of the shadows then and said, "You sure know how to handle them, Mr. Gress."

The circus man laughed and cracked his whip.

Then he turned in the direction of the cage and yelled, "I'M GONNA MAKE A NIGGER OUT OF YA YET, GHOUL!"

CHAPTER 18

WO days after their journey to the circus Ebb had designs on revisiting the same. However, he had heard nothing from Bo and assumed that Bo was being punished for excessive circus fervor. Ebb spent the day reminiscing about their circus adventure when Topper appeared.

"Ebb, did you hear about Moll Legg Island bein' robbed?" Topper, exhausted and out of breath, flopped down on the soft straw bed Ebb had spread out for Honker under the cherry tree. He lay motionless, his long wheezes leading one to believe that he was surely about to die.

"Robbed!" Ebb turned his head attentively toward Top, but, recognizing his loss of restraint, quickly checked himself and continued playing tag with a bewildered ladybug.

Topper, seeing that his efforts at getting attention were not fully appreciated, sat straight up against the old gnarled tree and after some serious forethought pronounced the words that moved Ebb to lower his brow and stare unbelievingly in his direction.

"My dad just come back from town. He says they're all excited 'cus Lare come back from Moll Legg for the sheriff. Lare found a dead body!"

Ebb's ears twitched. He picked up a stick of straw and excitedly bit the stem, still trying to keep his air of disinterest. "So what?" Ebb said. "People find bodies all the time."

"Yeah, but not with the graves dug up!"

Ebb's ears twitched again. "Dug up—you sure?"

"Sure, I'm sure. Lare told 'em."

Without hesitation, Ebb and Top rushed down to Periwinkle Pier. Ebb's old and leaking rowboat floated half-hidden, half-submerged beneath the barnacled quay. The word *Hardhead* was unmistakably imprinted on the gunwale in bright, uneven red letters. With unfaltering zeal and determination, they bailed out the old boat and quickly started for Talbot's landing, rowing harder than usual and intermittently keeping their toes busy plugging seep holes. The old skiff cut smooth, glassy rivulets in her wake as they made way toward Cove Point. The invincible flies bit fiercely and let blood, easing the boredom and distracting from the gnawing pain associated with the boys' task of rowing. The boat yawed to port, to starboard, to port. When they finally arrived at Talbot's pier, water had found its mark as Ebb and Top half rowed and half swam to the shallow base. They quickly jumped out of *Hardhead* into a foot of water and let the skiff settle to the sand.

An hour had passed since the gathering in Talbot's restaurant. All the shops were closed. Clusters of people talked and drank or played one-armed bandits. Ebb and Topper sat watchfully on the floor in back of the restaurant by the magazine rack, occasionally glancing at the "No Minors Allowed" sign. Three big fans slowly rotated. The sweet, smooth air was heavy with the smell of seaweed. Restlessly, Ebb got to his feet.

"How 'bout a Coke?"

Just as Top looked about, Jeff Durham, the town's grocer, charged through the double doors of the bar-restaurant and shouted, "He's comin'!"

Everyone moved toward the doorway. Some people burst out into the day and stood on the pier. The women stood back under the eaves. Lare's boat appeared in the distance, seemingly suspended in time. The sun shone brighter and lit up a cumulus bank of fog which, in the distance, stood like a massive white mountain. The low, whining sound of Lare's small outboard motor pierced the quiet as the approaching boat glided slowly over the slack, glassy water. Moments which seemed like hours slowly passed. As Lare came closer, it became apparent that he towed something resembling a huge fish behind his boat. It was the body, twisting and occasionally plunging beneath the water's surface— like something alive and very angry.

At a proper distance, slowly, Lare cut off his engine and let the boat move of its own momentum to the dock. No one said a word. The body sank slowly in the water, its head coming to rest face down in the shallow seaweed. The feet were tied with rope and fastened to the stern board. The arms and hands were outstretched —fingers spread, gray and chalky. Minnows nibbled at the shredded skin.

"Who is it?" Mr. Talbot asked. He stepped forward to give Lare a hand. Ben Morris, the iceman, did the same.

"I can't tell too much," Lare answered. "His face and most of his body is eaten away."

"Ed, a colored family at Shanty got a son missin'." Ben Morris knelt down for a closer look at the corpse. "I don't know how true it is, but there's rumor that we've got a madman who escaped from that circus some two days ago. . . . What do you think?"

Lare glanced back at the body. "Could be," he said skeptically. "I ain't really noticed anything. I got off that island as fast as I could. There's a grave open."

"A grave open!" Mr. Morris stood back, his mouth agape.

119

Lare nodded his head. "As sure as I'm sittin' here," he said, "there's a grave dug up." He toyed with the rope holding the burdened corpse.

By noon several cars cluttered Solomons Road. The sheriff's prussian-blue Mercury sat parked in the middle of the road in front of Talbot's restaurant, its yellow light rotating—flashing. Ebb, Fasso and Top stood outside the crowded cafe listening from between the big, swinging doors. Sheriff Persom, Mr. Lare and Fess had returned from another trip to the burial mounds of Moll Legg Island. Excitement stirred the air, and such stories were told and retold as to enliven the imagination and tongue of the most reticent observer. In due time, the deep, resonant voice of Sheriff Persom gradually took control.

"QUIET!—QUIET! We can't do nothin' till everyone's QUIET!"

Slowly, the drone of the fans became noticeably audible. The sheriff jumped up onto a small, rounded table, but lost his footing and careened into the opposite side of the crowd. In disbelief and with some misgiving, the people good-naturedly picked him up by the shoulders and legs and placed him back up on the table.

"God damn!" the sheriff grumbled. He arched his neck and dusted off his hat. Seized with injured dignity, he shouted, "Where the hell is Doc Cobb?"

No one said a word until Mr. Talbot answered from behind the bar. "He's over to St. Marys County, Sheriff."

"Give him a call, would you, Bill—Cherby . . . is Cherby here?"

Nobody answered.

"God damn—where is Cherby? Henderson!" the sheriff shouted.

Mr. Henderson raised his hand.

120

"John, would you take two men and wrap that body up in somethin' and put 'em in the icehouse."

As Henderson turned to leave, the sheriff held up both of his hands signaling for everybody to listen.

"Before any of you go," he said, "it's my duty to warn ALL of you. None of you is to leave this county till we find out what's goin' on here. Lare, me and Fess just came back from Moll Legg Island. Like Lare says, a grave's been dug up. Not only that, but all the graves on the island's been tampered with."

A commotion started up in the crowd. Somebody yelled, "It's that ghoul!"

Everyone looked anxiously back to the sheriff. Miss Damily, a spinster of the town, faintly muttered, "Oh, God!" Joe Bickles and "Moon" Mullen started for the swinging doors.

"Hold on! Hold on!" the sheriff yelled desperately.

"Hold on for what?" Bickles shouted back angrily. "It don't take too much thinkin' to understand who this ghoul might eat next." The words, catalytic in their fervor, stunned the crowd. En masse, they swept toward the doors.

"God damnation—HOLD ON!" the sheriff shouted. Then, clearing his throat and lowering his voice, he continued. "We're not gonna get anywhere if we don't all stick together and work this thing out together! Now, most of you know—or you should know—that there's a rumor goin' around this town that there's a madman loose; a ghoul they call him, who went crazy and escaped from the circus that's in Prince Frederick. Now, it ain't rumor that there was a man they called a ghoul at the circus. And it ain't a rumor that he's not there now. But it don't go on to say he's a madman, or a killer or anything of that sort.

"The graves are robbed, that's something. There's a body on ice in the back room, that's something else.

Now, I've already sent for help from the neighboring counties to put on a search. And that's what we've got to do till we find the man who the circus people says is a nigger—a dangerous nigger! They say he's six foot tall—maybe more. What he's wearing they don't know. Is anybody here seen this ghoul or this colored man?"

"I saw 'em!" Jim Stokes raised his hand. "And I wouldn't want to tangle with him."

"That's right, Sheriff," Judd Davis added excitedly. "He ain't for tangling! It was the bloodiest thing I've ever seen when I saw 'em in a killing match. He's lightin' fast and must have shark's teeth. He looks a dead man 'emself. He's got little red eyes . . . and moldy skin. Awful!"

The sheriff nervously loosened his collar and shifted his weight to his left foot. The din was momentarily broken by the noise of a slot machine's mechanical drums as they revolved and fell into place. Alarmed by the intrusion, the sheriff hesitated and, dazed, mentally searched for the appropriate answer.

"God damn!" The sheriff shook his head in doubt. "I don't know. Who ever let that son-of-a-bitch loose . . . The nigger, ghoul, whatever! He didn't escape himself. They told me . . ."

"I've got to take a leak." Ebb grimaced and hurried inside toward the men's room.

"Yeah, me too." Fasso clumsily followed Ebb through the door marked "Bucks." "Boy, this is scary! I didn't . . ." Ebb and Fasso both confronted the familiar open trough at the same time and immediately sought the privacy of the enclosed toilet. However, the appearance under the door of two tennis shoes, stemmed by white, thin legs, changed their minds. Embarrassed, Ebb hesitantly approached the urinal as did Fasso, both stumbling to unbutton their flies.

122

"Damn, I thought I had to go," Ebb quibbled. "I guess I don't now."

"Naw, me neither," retorted Fasso.

Awkwardly, they bumped into each other as they quickly approached the door.

Ebb had just exited when he heard somebody say "lock on his cage," and saw Stokes start out the door again.

"Stokes!" The sheriff directed his forefinger at the man. "I'm gonna hafta deputize you, Stokes, so wait on." Stokes stopped short at the door. Without turning, he stood and listened.

"I'm gonna hafta deputize all of you men," the sheriff continued. "After that, I want you all to go home and bring the women and children into town. You folks who have room and wouldn't mind havin' company for a night or two, please accommodate your neighbor. You men bring your guns. We'll meet back here at three o'clock.

"Now, one more thing." Sheriff Persom looked particularly at Syrus Sam as he spoke. Syrus was a good-natured, old black man who worked for the Timothy Richmond Crab House. He had worked there for forty-two years.

"Syrus tells me Mrs. Bodecker, a colored lady at Shanty, hasn't seen her son for two days. Mr. Morris and Syrus both think the body Lare found is one and the same, William Bodecker, called Bo by some. Any of you know . . ."

"Bo . . . Bodecker. BO!"—Ebb's head swam with illusions. He became dizzy and sought the shadows of the porch and sank despondently to the floor. Slowly he inched his way to the wall. The name "Bo" rang unmercifully in his ears, rending surrealistic waves of seawater, slapping relentlessly against his mind's eye,

123

and flowing profusely into a fathomless abyss of restless, unsaid affection.

"Saw grass. SHARP." He envisioned Bo's body swirling around and around in an ethereal tidal pool, his legs swinging free and listless. His body. Dead.

Thoughts. Strange, irrelevant thoughts, continued to flood his mind.

"Bo, d'you like girls?"

"Girls!"

"I seen one . . . I seen one naked! She's got hair right here!"

Wham! Two red swinging doors bounced against the outside wall. Ebb looked up. There stood the sheriff before him, big and shining clean.

". . . a, you know Bo, son?"

Scared and surprised, Ebb stammered, "Nnnnnnn . . . na . . . na . . . not much, sir."

"When was the last time you saw the boy, son?"

Ebb hung his head in embarrassment, as tears filled his eyes.

"Well, son?" the sheriff said impatiently.

"On the river," Ebb managed to murmur.

"When?"

"When the drum come."

"You haven't seen 'em since?"

Ebb slowly rose and abruptly turned from the sheriff without a word. He walked to the nearest corner of Talbot's restaurant and hid his face in remorse. Fasso and Top came out from their hiding and stood watchfully at his back.

"What's wrong, Ebb?" Top asked respectfully.

People rushed out of the restaurant onto the boardwalk and down to the dusty road.

"One less nigger here ain't gonna hurt none," came a voice in the crowd.

124

"Maybe we ought to leave this ghoul alone. He might eat up all the niggers," said another.

Laughter faded away in the roar of departing cars.

CHAPTER 19

ARLY the next morning, Doc Cobb's boat moved steadily across the calm Patuxent River toward the buttressed shore of Talbot's landing. Only the drone of the old ten-horsepower Johnson engine broke the peaceful silence. As the boat angled toward the lead piling, Doc Cobb grabbed for the motor grip, but was too late to lift the propeller free of the thick bed of seaweed. The motor sputtered once and died. Slowly, the boat drifted toward the pier. The sun was warm. Sea gulls stood one-legged and lazy on the barnacled pilings by the icehouse. The street was empty.

Doc Cobb climbed carefully onto the wharf and took several short, steady steps to the side of the pier. He always enjoyed the early morning quiet. Sometimes he would be enjoying this remote quietness so much that he would forget to tie his boat to the dock. This was one such morning. He turned and looked down the road toward Jim Talbot's restaurant. He was accustomed to seeing Mr. Poe or Mr. Timothy sitting on the front store bench. But what caught his eye this morning were the eleven boats anchored carelessly at the edge of Tigg's Boat House. Most unusual for a Tuesday morning. Slipping a small silver flask from inside his shirt, Doc Cobb took a leisurely swig and started off for Talbot's restaurant.

Five miles away, four weary men stood staring silently down the small embankment at Jefferson's Slough. The river had ebbed considerably. The body of a black man lay high on its bank. The men showed little grief. Except for Jess Young. Jess cried softly and shook his head. Two empty, red pumpkin-ball shotgun shells lay at his feet.

As though paralyzed by the realization of their own mortality, no one made a move toward the dying man. As the tidal ridge turned white and dry from the hot sun, the intense heat seared the black man's parched, mud-caked skin much the same. A thin, dark trickle of blood oozed from the corners of the man's mouth and dropped to the sediment. Slowly, his big, cracked lips opened. But his words slipped out unnoticed; lost forever to the drone of flies and the silence of death. His eyes stared blank to the sun. It was the ghoul man.

CHAPTER 20

FTER the shooting, Solomons Island changed from a sleepy, peaceful country town into a bustling, chaotic news haven. At least that's the way it appeared to the people of Solomons. The topic of the day which was discussed with fervor was the pending investigation and the coming of the county coroner.

Beginning at 9:30 a.m. on Wednesday, Mrs. Talbot called every local resident. A gentleman from Washington, D.C., had called to reserve every available sleeping space he could—one dollar in advance for each booking. Such an event precluded any commercial rentals from Solomons Island to Prince Frederick and spurred the townspeople to rent out rooms in their homes. By the time the coroner came, "foreigners" were living in barns and shacks "not suited for a dog." Because of the fire hazard, some local folk didn't take to the city folk setting up house in their barns. But the town's council was most hospitable and suggested that such available space be set up like dormitories: Board —$10.00 a week.

Then came the cars. One by one they passed in procession over the land bridge until they abruptly came to a stop. The passengers sat patiently while Deputy Max Crocker tried in vain to unravel the congestion at the other end of the only road in Solomons. Ebb and Top sat on top of the roof of Captain Tigg's Boat House. It was all very amusing to them. They counted cars and took stock of the passengers.

"It was better than any sideshow I'd ever seen," Ebb would later say. "Those people were crazy. They cussed and blowed their horns—spittin' and everything. You would of swore that this here island was one big smoke engine ready to take off."

Top, in his enthusiasm, showed Mr. Poe a handful of coins—dimes and nickels. They both grinned and commenced to tell Mr. Poe of their cunning enterprise fashioned after Jimmy Parker's luck.

"This man in a black Hudson asked Jimmy if he knew of a place to park. Well," Top shrugged his shoulders, "all Jimmy done was take him to his place and tell him to park in the field. The man gave him a nickel, so, that's what *we* been doin'! Everybody done it!"

The boys laughed and rolled back on their heels. They hadn't told Poe all that went on, but he knew by the gleam in their eyes that the fun had only begun.

The food and liquor stores swelled with business and excitement. The swinging doors to Talbot's bar were in constant motion and the one-armed bandit's mechanical pulse, set off by the ringing of a winning bell, gave the illusion of a carnival atmosphere. Ebb said, "Sounds filtered through the noise, and things were said that would of made a mule's ears drop off. Couldn't even hear the cash register ring."

This was also a time that the boys wished they had had Billy Talbot's job selling newspapers. No sooner would he get a new stack of papers to sell than he would rush into Talbot's bar and holler "Newspaper— get your daily newspaper! KILLER! KILLER!

KILLER!" Then he would run back outside and wait for the crowd. He made a pocketful of change.

When Ebb went home that night, his Grandma Kellum was standing at the window. That was unusual for her. But there she was and Ebb knew that meant exceptional trouble. As Ebb described the occasion:

> She stood like a sulking chicken, staring at the curtain, not saying a word. She didn't look at me once till I asked if she's dying, not to be disrespectful, because that's the way she does sometimes. Then I saw that she had been crying—and that made me feel awful bad.
>
> "What you cryin' for, Gram?" I said it as apologetic as I was.
>
> She turned and looked down at me. She wiped her eyes with her napkin and blew her nose.
>
> "What's got into you, Chase?" She dimmed her eyes and looked at me hard from under those bushy, white eyebrows.
>
> I suspected that the trouble was the cherry throwin'. It was custom for me and Top to skim the roofs of cars with cherries. Only this day one of those cherries hit a man aside his face and stopped him cold. He jumped out of that automobile and swat his face like somethin' bit him. Then looking back in the car he saw that cherry. That's when me and Top ran as fast as we could. I was sure he seen us.
>
> "I didn't throw it, Gram!—Honest, I didn't!" Confessin' ain't one of my strong points. She wrinkled her brow and sat down on the sofa.
>
> "Throw what?" she asked.
>
> I looked straight into her eyes and stood stonestruck. "Throw anything," I hedged.
>
> "That's right, throw anything?" she repeated. She was good at the game. She knew that some-

thing was up. But she didn't meddle this time. She held out a piece of paper and shook it in front of me.

"This is from the sheriff!"

"From the sheriff!" I stared at that piece of paper and watched every move she made with it. She wiped her eyes again and commenced to read, "Coroner's Subpoena for Witness." She stopped long enough to see if I was uncomfortable, then she continued.

"The people of the State of Maryland send greetings to Mr. Chase Ezekiel Kellum. . . ." She looked up and repeated the name in a soft, broken voice. Once she got her composure, she was all right. "We command you . . ."

"Mister Chase Ezekiel Kellum." The name rang in my ears. "Mister ain't me," I said confidently.

"This 'Mister' is for sure you," she said.

I felt ten feet tall and twice as scared. "What's it mean?" I asked.

"It means that you have got involved in something that is VERY WRONG. The sheriff wants to find out who . . ."

"I don't know anything, Gram. Honest!"

"They *think* you do or they wouldn't be asking your presence at this inquiry."

Grandma Kellum didn't cry anymore. But it was no time before her praying garments started to rustle and her praying voice started out deep and loud. She waved her hands over my head and prayed. The ceremony was long and made me most tired. I near fell asleep. But Gram kept on. She made sure the devil weren't there, and when she was certain, she said in a stern voice, "Now, you tell me what you know about this poor man who was shot last week, and about that dead boy they found in the river."

CHAPTER 21

HE inquest began early the 4th of August, 1949. The Star of the Sea schoolhouse, where it was held, was packed. People pushed into the foyer despite efforts to keep it clear. Occasionally a head was seen bobbing up and down at the window as some small boy tried persistently to keep a foothold on the outside trim of the building. The petunias that the good Sister Julia had so carefully grown were trampled. The small white fence that had surrounded them was torn up and laid to the side.

For Ebb, it was all very frightening. Yet he felt a kind of satisfaction in the presence of so much attention and mystery. He sat attentively in the second row of seats with his Grandma Kellum and Uncle Elton. The change in the schoolhouse was strange to him. Nothing was the same, except for the blackboard. And even that had an unnatural, coal-black cleanness. The two new erasers that were side by side on the mantel mesmerized him for a moment. Briefly his mind was at peace.

The teacher's desk was still in the center of a platform in the front of the room. Two long oak tables had been placed at right angles on either side. A small utility table was set in front and to the side of the platform. Ebb relaxed somewhat in seeing Jimmy Harris' chewing gum still stuck to the underside of the teacher's desk.

A back door into the cloak room suddenly opened. As four men stepped into the open room, the audience felt a mixture of awe and curiosity. The new arrivals sat down in their seats and began to chat leisurely amongst themselves. The front seat remained empty, preserving the reverence of the occasion. Ebb recognized Sheriff Persom and Mayor Talbot but was unfamiliar with the other two men. Unaccustomed to such proceedings, he sat back in his seat and watched attentively. Shortly, the door opened again. Such a silence settled upon the panel that Ebb had visions of seeing the Lord himself. Then a man with no more presence than a scarecrow stepped into the room.

"Dr. James D. Wadsworth. Everyone please stand."

The crowd rose together as a tall, lean man dressed in a black suit entered the room. He went straight to the center desk and stood solemnly behind the chair. The man reminded Ebb of the mean old bearded rooster on the Jeffersons' farm—"never allowing an inch —always strutting proud." Ebb strained his eyes in curiosity. He had seen this man moments before, talking to Mr. Bone about the price of fish. The coroner adjusted his glasses and said gruffly, "Ladies and gentlemen—this is not a trial. This is a coroner's inquest to determine evidence as to the death of Mr. Chickabee Wilson. While these proceedings are informal, the rules of court will be observed. We will now say the Lord's Prayer."

To Ebb, the coroner's manner of speech was bad— and his manners worse. Once the prayer was finished, the coroner sat down before the ladies did! Unforgivable to a Kellum.

The coroner's appearance behind the desk was comical. Not only did he discover his legs were too long for the desk, but his unusually long arms dwarfed its top. Attempting to conceal his embarrassment, he moved his chair away from the desk as if to inspect the platform. Then he folded his arms and nodded his head. Sheriff Persom stood and read the name of Mr. Silas Lare from a roster. The inquest had begun.

Mr. Lare, who had been standing in the back of the room, hurriedly came forward with long strides down the middle aisle. He took the oath "to tell the truth and nothing but the truth" and quickly sat down in the side chair. He smiled as always.

The coroner looked over at him. "Mr. Lare, would you please state your full name, address and occupation," he asked.

Mr. Lare looked from right to left. He had practiced several times at home. "My name is Silas Edward Lare. I live on Spot Lane on Solomons Island. And my occupation is mostly fishin'." He said it proudly. And he was proud.

The coroner sat patiently and waited for Mr. Lare to say more. But he said nothing more until the need to break the silence led him to add, "I farm, too."

But the words were barely audible over the simultaneous intrusion of Coroner Wadsworth's question. "Mr. Lare, on July 27th of this year, you brought in a body to Talbot's wharf. Would you tell us where you found the body and any circumstances that will give us information as to its identity?"

The question stirred Mr. Lare. He shifted in his seat and stared thoughtfully out in the direction of the river. "I remember seein' that body, Mr. Judge," he answered slowly, "I remember seein' that body . . ."

Mr. Lare shook his head absentmindedly and looked apologetically back up at the coroner.

134

"To tell the truth," he continued, "the only thing I really seen was somethin' floatin'. Just floatin'. I didn't suspect it was anything. But it looked odd! It was foggy and there I was in my boat coming slow off Cedar Point. The tide was moving out right steady and calm. I near passed the body. It was to starboard and from here to . . ." Mr. Lare looked around the room and pointed to the back window. "That window!" he said. "Right close to 'bout where that window is. It weren't far, but it was hard seein' in the fog. I looked in front of me anyway. I swerved the boat and came close to the floatin' thing. Then I seen it was a body. I didn't believe it! I turned the boat around and went back. Sure enough. There was that dead boy floatin' face down with a big blue crab hangin' onto his head. He didn't even look human. The crabs, and whatever, had near peeled 'em. It weren't till I put the rope to his legs that I seen it's a nigger. That's it. I just towed 'em back here."

"Was there any clothing on the body?" the coroner asked.

"Yes, sir. Blue pants and a shirt." Mr. Lare nodded his head with certainty.

"From what direction do you think he might have floated?"

Mr. Lare pinched his chin and squinted his eyes. He stood up and walked over to the teacher's desk. He pointed to a white card the coroner had placed on the right side of the desk and said, "Here's Point Patience, Judge. This is . . ." Before he got to Cedar Point, Coroner Wadsworth directed Sheriff Persom to give Mr. Lare some chalk. Mr. Lare commenced to draw what he was describing on the blackboard. As they were familiar to most of the river people, he drew Sandy Point, Town Point and Drum Point as the main reference points.

"As I said," Mr. Lare continued, "the tide was movin' out pretty steady. It was close to 7:30 that morning. Full ebb came about 9:00 or 10:00.

"It coulda come from any one of them places, but bein' as it was to my starboard, it mighta come from Drum Point more so than the others."

Mr. Lare pointed to the location and continued the chalk line up the blackboard to a spot where he pressed, leaving a bold, white dot. He wrote "Solomons."

A fat man with a big, black graphic camera catwalked up to the front of the room and lay on the floor in front of the platform. Everybody saw him except the coroner, who was concentrating on what Mr. Lare was saying. Bemused, Silas stared straight at the man. He squinted his eyes.

"Well," he hesitated. As he went to point to Drum Point, a blinding white flash lit up the front of the room. Mr. Lare fell over backwards and rolled sideways off the platform. The panel put their arms over their eyes.

The coroner sat momentarily blinded. Stunned by this intrusion, he unfolded his arms and held on to the desk with uncertain hands. As soon as his vision returned, he jumped from his seat and leaned over the desk to see the cameraman. Then he said with peculiar calmness, "Please, sir. After the inquest. No more pictures now."

The stranger rolled onto his back with amazing agility, rocked to his feet and walked calmly out of the schoolhouse.

"Continue, Mr. Lare," the coroner encouraged. Slowly, he sat down again, all the while keeping a watchful eye on the doorway.

"Well, that's it, Mr. Judge. I towed 'em in to Talbot's pier." Mr. Lare stretched his neck and looked at the coroner.

136

"Mr. Lare, do you recall anybody saying who it was?" the coroner asked.

Mr. Lare thought for a minute. "Bodecker. William Bodecker."

Ebb suddenly felt sick to his stomach and dizzy in his head. The room was hot and stuffy. The sheriff called Mr. P. Gress as the next witness.

"Mr. Gress, do you have a first or middle name?" the coroner asked.

"Nope, just 'P.' "

It was the circus man. He was dressed handsomely in his circus togs. Ebb fancied the white silk shirt and the light brown ascot. He marveled even more at his spit-shined boots.

"What is your position, Mr. Gress?"

"I'm a foreman for the Barnum and Bailey Circus."

"You supervise the tent work, the feeding of the animals, the paying of the men, is that right?"

"Not the paying of the men—just the supervision of the manual labor."

"Do you have anything to do with the entertainment part of the circus?"

"Anybody who works with the circus has something to do with a little bit of everything."

"You are an entertainer then?"

"No, I'm not an entertainer as entertainers go," the circus man said. He chuckled to himself. "Just in a fix," he added. "Sometimes a clown. Sometimes a lion trainer. That's the way the circus is. You've got to be a jack-of-all-trades if you want a job."

"Even as a ghoul?"

"Even as a ghoul," the circus man answered.

"Mr. Gress, who was Mr. Chickabee Wilson?"

"Mr. Chickabee Wilson. He was a colored man. A good, hard-working colored man who worked for the circus."

137

"What kind of work did he do?"

"He did the kind of work most of us did. Like I told you, anybody who works for the circus does everything."

"You mean even substituting as a ghoul?"

Mr. Gress slid uncomfortably back in his chair. He crossed his feet and nervously pulled on his pants leg. Finally he said, "If we needed a ghoul, then somebody would be the ghoul." Fragments of straw and bits of manure fell from his boots to the floor as he sat up straight.

"Were you ever the ghoul, Mr. Gress?" the coroner asked.

Mr. Gress shook his head. "Never!"

"Didn't that job suit you?"

"Nope."

After an uncomfortable length of time passed, Mr. Gress looked up at the coroner. But the coroner said nothing. He just stared back at Mr. Gress.

"Mr. Wadsworth," Gress finally said, "as foreman of a circus, my work keeps me too busy to be concerned about who is, or who is not, to be the circus ghoul. Whoever wants to be the ghoul at that time is the ghoul!"

"How many different ghouls have you had during this year, Mr. Gress?" asked the coroner.

Mr. Gress uncrossed his feet and scratched his leg. "One," he said.

Coroner Wadsworth asked Mr. Gress to repeat his answer.

"We had only one ghoul this year!" Gress retorted.

"That was Mr. Chickabee Wilson?" the coroner asked.

"Yes, that was Mr. Wilson."

"Wasn't that unusual?" Coroner Wadsworth glanced over the rim of his glasses and stroked his beard.

138

"No, like I said. If somebody wanted to be a ghoul, then we let 'em be a ghoul."

"Who was the ghoul before Mr. Wilson?"

"A ummmmmm . . . a Mr. Cavanaugh."

"Was he employed in any other capacity?"

"He was a rigger."

"Where is Mr. Cavanaugh now?"

"I don't know." Mr. Gress turned to the coroner and shook his head. "I don't know."

"Was Mr. Cavanaugh a colored man?"

"Yes, matter of fact, he was." Gress reddened with anger.

"How many different ghouls have you had?"

". . . 'bout four or five. We started this show last season."

"How many Negroes acted as ghouls?" The coroner, seemingly satisfied with his line of questioning, took a drink of water and patiently waited for Gress to answer.

Boldly, Gress turned in his seat and said blatantly, "A ghoul's a nigger, Mr. Wadsworth. They was all niggers that I hired."

Almost everybody laughed. Except Mrs. Bodecker and Jonas. Mr. Gress took advantage of the situation and asked, "Have you ever seen a ghoul, Mr. Wadsworth? If you haven't, you've been missin' a mighty fine show. Why, a nigger makes the best ghoul right off, 'cus he's black!"

With that, people laughed until they cried. The coroner swung his mallet down hard.

The schoolhouse was quiet again. Coroner Wadsworth removed his glasses and wiped his forehead. He sat back in his chair and nervously tapped on his mallet.

He helplessly looked down at Gress and asked, "What does a ghoul do in a circus, Mr. Gress?"

139

Mr. Gress shrugged his shoulders. "He's an entertainer, like I said. What more can I say?"

"What kind of entertainer?" Coroner Wadsworth directed his question sharply and directly.

"What kind of entertainer?" Mr. Gress repeated the question. He scratched his head. "Well, you might say he makes out to be some kind of a monster who eats flesh. That's what a ghoul *is*, you know. He robs graves and eats dead people."

"Is that what this circus ghoul did?" the coroner asked.

"He didn't eat dead people. They're hard to come by," the circus man snickered. "Although," he hesitated, "it looks like he done found himself a home here in Solomons."

"That did it," Ebb recalled, "Grandma Kellum farted right out and the whole schoolhouse shook with laughter. The coroner stood up and started banging his mallet down hard across the top of the desk. Suddenly the mallet flew out of his hand, and went sliding across the floor. Nat Krammer, a visitor from Wachapreague, Virginia, couldn't stop from laughing. He jumped up and fought his way out the schoolhouse."

The coroner managed to retrieve his mallet and addressed the audience in both anger and disappointment. His reprimand was severe: "For a matter as serious as this, I am dismayed at the attitude of this . . . this group. If there is another outburst of this nature during these sessions, questioning will be held without an audience!" Unmoved by "such scoldin'," Gress grinned confidently and took his leave.

CHAPTER 22

SHERIFF PERSOM called old Fess Dodrill to the chair. People moved back in their seats and shied away from the aisle. No one could blame them. The only time anyone ever saw Fess was when someone died. And such occasions were by no means coincidental. He was the official gravedigger. And, according to the townspeople, no one was better at the job.

"Give 'em somethin' ta do with his hands," Mr. Poe would say. "Why Old Fess'd do a better job than most men. Why d'ya think they call 'em in for gravediggin'? 'Cus he does a darn good job, that's why! He don't raise no fuss or anything! He just goes ahead and does it. When he tells you he done it, you know he done it good."

However, all these compliments were of little help to Fess's reputation. People described him as hideous and repulsive—the "wolf man of Calvert County." No one ever noticed his kindness and gentleness.

Fess slowly walked forward and sat down. He was as nervous as a game hen and chewed his gums more than usual. His protruding lips had open scabs of dried blood. Beady red eyes sulked beneath heavy black eyebrows. His curved fingernails were long and dirty. All the stories Ebb had heard about Fess stirred his imagination.

As the tension in the schoolroom eased, Coroner Wadsworth relaxed and pushed his chair gradually back toward the blackboard. However, judging by the twitching of his nose, the move was intended to put him a good smelling distance away from Fess.

"Mr. Dodrill, you are the gravedigger of this town, are you not?" Coroner Wadsworth asked looking apprehensively at Fess.

"Yes . . . yes, sir," Fess admitted after much consideration.

"You dug all the graves on . . ." Coroner Wadsworth glanced down at a piece of yellow paper on the desk. "You dug all the graves on Moll Legg Island?" People stirred in their seats. Ebb looked fearfully at Fess. He saw all the devils of Moll Legg sitting and waiting.

Moll Legg Island had a fearsome reputation for all that was evil. One sultry night a land mass appeared suddenly in the middle of the river splitting the channel one mile north/south, its width a tenth that distance. Some called it a sandbar, others an island. It was cursed and shunned. Four months after the island emerged, a black man was found dead on its sands. Those who found him said that he had drowned. But Doc Cobb was skeptical. They had dragged the poor soul to the dock to be identified but nobody came to claim his remains. So they dragged him back out to the island and buried him there. Since then, anybody found dead who didn't have kin was buried on Moll Legg. As Ebb would have one believe, "Nobody goes there 'ceptin' Sheriff Persom, Doc Cobb and Old Fess. It's bare as any bones I suspect is there."

Fess remained silent until the coroner repeated his name. "Were you the gravedigger for all those graves, Mr. Dodrill?" Old Fess nodded his head that he was,

142

but the coroner asked him politely for a verbal "yes" or "no."

"Is anyone with you when you lower those mortals to their rest?" Coroner Wadsworth asked.

"Mor . . . mor . . ." Fess stammered. He looked quizzically up at the coroner.

"The people you buried, Mr. Fess." The coroner was patient. "Does anyone stay with you while these people are buried?"

"No, s-s-s-sir. Th . . . they ne-ver stayed." Fess paused. "Da . . . Doc Cobb an-n-n da sher . . . sheriff. Th . . . they only come ba . . . back to see tha . . . that the grave's right."

Fess smiled and said proudly, "Th . . . they s-said, I-I-I-m right."

"Mr. Dodrill, how often do you go out to Moll Legg Island?"

Fess shrugged his shoulders. "Ev . . . ev-ry da . . . day," he said.

"Every day!"

"Ye . . . yessir. I che . . . check ta see ev-ev-thing's right."

"Did you ever notice anything unusual?"

Fess paused a moment.

"Did you ever notice the dirt or sand laid differently —anything out of order from how you kept it? Were the graves always the way you left them?"

Fess began to show the first signs of emotion. Waves of sorrow and anger moved across his contorted face.

"Ye . . . yessir. A . . . a . . . 'ceptin' af . . . aft' a stormmmm; a win . . . win . . . wind." Fess nodded his head. His eyes shifted to a distant object. Coroner Wadsworth, beginning to tire of Fess's ways, raised his voice impatiently.

"MR. DODRILL!"

143

Fess, unmoved by the coroner's abruptness, raised his head and said, "All . . . always th . . . the same."

Ebb, mesmerized by Fess's slowness and dulled by the heat of the day, sluggishly bobbed his head, when he heard his name called: "MISTER CHASE KELLUM."

Before the shock had a chance to settle, his Grandma Kellum had pushed him up and out of the seat. Startled, he hesitantly walked forward. In his trance, he saw nothing and heard only the incredibly loud echo of his shoes against the floorboards. He hoped right then as deeply as he could that "niggers never come into my life again." As he approached the coroner, he first calmed to see Mrs. Bodecker sitting big before his eyes. Then as he turned his head away, shame filled his thoughts in that he hadn't taken the responsibility to meet her as "Bo's ma." It was the first time that he had ever seen her so close.

Coroner Wadsworth searched through his papers. Without looking up he said in a friendly tone, "How are you today, Mr. Kellum?"

Ebb looked up. He was thoroughly surprised to see the coroner smiling down at him. "Fine, thank ya," Ebb said without hesitation. The promptness of his reply surprised even him.

"I read your poem, Mr. Kellum. A fine piece of literature!"

Ebb noticed some of the people in the audience smile, especially his grandma. He was proud and glad that the coroner remembered the poem.

"How old are you, son?"

"Eleven." Ebb thought that question was much easier than what Fess had to answer to.

"Eleven, hummmmmm. You're a pretty big boy for eleven. Are you on the football team?"

"No," Ebb answered, embarrassed that he wasn't.

"What's your occupation, son?"

144

"Occupation?" This question seemed peculiar to Ebb.

"Do you have a working job?"

"School. A . . . a huntin', fishin'—crabbin'!" The coroner thought Ebb had finished, and started to ask another question only to be interrupted by Ebb's enthusiasm.

"Trappin'," Ebb went on; then added, "skinnin'."

The coroner smiled. "You must keep pretty busy."

"Yes, sir!"

"Have you ever worked for the circus?"

"Yes, sir!"

"When did you work there, son?"

"More'n a week ago."

"How did you like working for the circus?"

Ebb thought that was a silly question. The coroner, sensing Ebb's thoughts, smiled and said, "What did you do when you worked for the circus?"

"Pulled the tents up."

"By yourself?" The audience laughed.

Ebb, having resigned himself to the coroner's naive discussion on the circus, said, "No," shaking his head in disbelief.

"Who helped you then?"

"Men. Circus men."

"Did Mr. Bodecker help you?"

"Mr. Bodecker?" Ebb gulped. His thoughts were becoming a mixture of fear and sadness.

"The boy called 'Bo'—did he help you pull up these tents?" Coroner Wadsworth continued.

It was strange to Ebb to hear Bo referred to as "Mister." He pinched his leg and said, "A little."

Ebb feeling the coroner's eyes burning into him looked up at him and continued. "He was there, that's all. He just come to pull the tent up with everybody else. We all got a ticket for it."

"You both got free tickets to the circus?"

145

"I guess so," Ebb said. "*I* did."

"Weren't you and Bo—Mr. Bodecker, good friends?"

Ebb looked out into the audience and saw his grandma and Uncle Kellum sitting there like proud eagles. His eyes burned with sadness. Slowly his vision dissolved into what Ebb described as "niggers, hundreds of midget niggers, all lookin' like Bo. They kicked and shouted and called Jonas by name, 'NIGGER, NIGGER—JONAS BLACK, NIGGER, NIGGER —JONAS.' " They shouted louder and faster till all he heard was Jonas' insane laughter ringing in his ears.

"You ain't a nigger . . ." Ebb's voice was barely audible.

"What did you say?" the coroner asked in surprise.

Ebb's eyes focused on his grandma and uncle again. "It was like they was neither here nor there—just staring and expecting nothing but what they was."

"No, sir," Ebb finally said, and wished God would strike him dead.

The sheriff called Mrs. Roselyn Bodecker as the next witness. Ebb went back to his seat and recalled that "half of the room seemed to get up at once." Mrs. Bodecker's swiftness in spite of her size took the coroner by surprise. She was dressed in faded black and looked sad, "the way fat people look sad," he said.

She walked as fast as a possum to the witness chair and sat down before they could give her the oath. She had a respectability about her that was common with the backwood country folk. Ebb envisioned his nanny, Martha, sitting there. He wanted to hug her. The coroner's mouth softened.

"Mrs. Bodecker, from the testimony given at this inquest, it has been suggested that the boy Mr. Lare found on the river is your son, William Bodecker." Coroner Wadsworth hesitated and after thoughtful con-

146

sideration asked, "Do you have any reason to believe that this boy, who you identified at Sheriff Persom's office, is not your son?"

Mrs. Bodecker looked mournfully at her other son, Jonas, and closed her eyes. "It him," she said softly.

The coroner leaned sympathetically toward her. "Pardon, Mrs. Bodecker?"

"It look like 'em. He ain't been home for da longest time." Her heavy, brown cheeks shook with emotion. She turned her head away and cried silently. She wiped her tears away with the back of her hand. Hers were kind, warm hands—full of love and work.

"It been a long time," she continued. "He was a nice boy. I treat 'em hard sometimes." She looked around and stared straight at Ebb. "He changed. He changed somethin'."

Her eyes were as deep as time to Ebb. Not mean, just sorry. Sorry for everything there was to be sorry for. Eyes that were the Patuxent, an eastern storm and a purple rainbow. Understanding eyes. Eyes that were a warm sun and a dead tree.

"Changed?" the coroner asked in surprise.

"Changed!" she said emphatically. She looked up at Coroner Wadsworth. "We all been friends in this town. Everybody treats us nice. People always brings us vegetables and things. Folks in town always been good to Jonas and Bo in givin' 'em work. We always got plenty."

Mrs. Bodecker then lapsed into silence until she said something that seemed very familiar to Ebb.

". . . I heard from . . . Bo was good. I let 'em play whenever he want. Only I didn't see 'em like I use ta. He kept everything to 'emself."

"Mrs. Bodecker, when was the last time you saw your son?"

"It was last Monday, a week. He'd been to da circus.

147

He was hungry and ate like I never seen 'em. He said he got somethin' to do and run out da house. I told 'em I didn't want 'em goin' out no more. But he had somethin' on his mind and he weren't hearin' me.

"Mr. Judge, he ain't like that. My boys is good boys. You ask anybody. Dey's hard workers and honest. Dey loves their ma and obey. But this time, my Bo . . . Somethin' get into 'em. I don't know what. He gone now."

Coroner Wadsworth listened intently, becoming so absorbed with what Mrs. Bodecker had said that he didn't hear her silence. But by the time he had cleared his throat, Mrs. Bodecker resumed.

"He'd never been nasty," she said, "even to an animal. One day he get nasty to my Jonas." Mrs. Bodecker looked lovingly at Jonas. She shook her head. "No more fishin', no more crabbin'," she continued. "Dey ain't been together for some time."

"Do you know why?" the coroner asked.

"I got suspicions, but I don't wanta say 'em," she said scornfully.

Coroner Wadsworth slowly rubbed the side of his face. "Mrs. Bodecker," he said, "your son may have been murdered. If you have suspicions, it might be of considerable help if you tell us."

Mrs. Bodecker hesitated. She rubbed her eyes and coughed nervously. "She was bein' stubborn, for sure," Ebb related.

"We can't help you, Mrs. Bodecker, until we have all the facts," said the coroner.

She leaned forward and opened her mouth to say something, but she didn't. Her whole body melted back into the seat. Coroner Wadsworth waited patiently. Suddenly, Mrs. Bodecker exploded with emotion. "It just don't take!"

The coroner looked down at Mrs. Bodecker and asked impatiently, "What don't take?"

148

"Somethin' just don't take," she answered in a low, hesitant voice.

Coroner Wadsworth hardened his voice and began to prod her with words until, in a desperate, angry, and direct statement, she said aloud, "BLACK FOLK BEIN' WITH WHITE FOLK JUST DON'T TAKE!"

The coroner squinted his eyes and cleared his throat again. The audience buzzed with talk until Mrs. Bodecker cried and said apologetically, "I don't know what I'm sayin', Judge. I worked for them people all my life."

Grandma Kellum turned mad red and looked as indignant as a caged bobcat. She whispered to Miss Damily, who sat next to her, all the while staring at Mrs. Bodecker with more malice and hate than Ebb had ever seen. Mrs. Bodecker looked fearfully up at the school ceiling.

"I know he in heaven," she cried. "I seen 'em." She raised her voice and repeated, "I *seen* 'em clear as day! His wings was gold. Gold like the sun. I seen 'em!"

"You saw your son, Mrs. Bodecker?" The coroner adjusted his glasses. Mrs. Bodecker took a deep breath. Her body trembled with emotion. Her eyes, red from weeping, stared with love.

"Yes, I seen 'em," she continued. "I seen 'em in Glory." She said it softly, gently.

"I dozed dat night in the 'honey-house.' The pine was whisperin'. Den, GOD COME! OH, GOD! GOD! LOVE GOD! HE COME! His voice from heaven wake me. It shook the house and scraped the walls. I looked out a knothole and seen my Bo right 'fore my eyes!" Mrs. Bodecker shook her head sadly and looked at the floor. "He changed. He looked old. He even got wings . . . wings big as anything—and bright! He crowed like a rooster and flowed away . . . he ain't no more . . ." Mrs. Bodecker got up slowly and confidently. Relaxed

149

in the conclusion of her story, she returned to her seat, as sad as she had left it.

A hush settled over the schoolhouse as the audience waited for the next witness to be called. Most had thought that the panel had run out of witnesses until the sheriff finally called Mr. Goodlittle. Mr. Goodlittle was the town barber. Elton Kellum claimed he was the worst haircutter there was and that chicken pluckers could do better. Mr. Goodlittle was as thin as a stick worm. His voice was high-pitched—his movements equally peculiar. He looked especially funny to Ebb today, although for no reason. Ebb bit his lip in order to keep from laughing. Finally he had to look away.

"Mr. Goodlittle." The coroner's voice unintentionally mimicked the barber's manner. This made Ebb want to laugh even more. His stomach began to hurt. He bit his tongue trying desperately to keep back the urge to burst into laughter.

"Yeah," Mr. Goodlittle replied.

Now tears came to Ebb's eyes. He leaned down and hid his face between his legs. Margie Kellum, trying to ignore his antics, nudged the boy smartly. However, this only made him laugh more. He laughed inwardly until he was exhausted. Mr. Goodlittle, in the meanwhile, told the coroner about the hunt.

". . . by Jefferson's Slough and walking north toward Miller's farm when this ugly, hunched-over darkie came out of the brush some fifty yards from where we was walking. He came sliding down the slope and started across the shallow with his arms uplifted and his palms outstretched. He didn't say a thing—not a thing—just walked toward us. Jess Young raised his gun—and when the nigger saw that, he stopped. Jess told 'em to stand where he was. But the nigger turned and started to go back. Jess told 'em to stop. But the nigger paid no heed and started runnin' like a chimpanzee or somethin'. Jess fired a shot in the mud to scare 'em, but the nigger had started up the slope. Before he got halfway up, Jess sighted his gun to wound him. Even at the distance, it weren't meant for no harm. The shot brought 'em down all right. He didn't move. And we knew he was the ghoul; he . . ." Before Mr. Goodlittle could finish, there was a big commotion in back of the schoolhouse. Mr. Goodlittle looked up and everybody turned to see what was happening. From out of the shadows came a deep, rich voice they knew only too well.

"I'm your killer, Dr. Wadsworth."

CHAPTER 23

N the doorway, silhouetted against the bright daylight, stood Doc Cobb. Steadying himself with one arm stiff to the doorjamb, he stared angrily back at all those staring his way. The shock of his sudden, silent appearance brought uneasiness to the gathering. As he walked slowly down the middle aisle, they could see that his condition was questionable. As he neared Coroner Wadsworth, he stopped short to where Mr. Goodlittle sat. Reaching for the witness chair and holding it tightly, he said in a sober voice, "I've got something needs sayin'!"

Mr. Goodlittle, unsure of what was happening, stood up from the witness chair and looked apprehensively at the coroner. Without asking, and indeed in a manner befitting a man of tactics, Doc Cobb quickly sat down in Goodlittle's place. His determination precluded his removal—and so he sat. Coroner Wadsworth hastily put on his glasses and looked at the intruder as if it was the first time he had noticed his presence. He could see by the doctor's posture and wearied face that the old man had had little sleep, and that he was deeply grieved. Doc Cobb wore his white suit, an outfit usually reserved for special summer events. The suit was badly

152

wrinkled and stained. His shirt collar stuck awkwardly from beneath his coat. The doctor rubbed his forehead with the palm of his hand and in a slow, direct voice said, "I robbed those graves, Dr. Wadsworth."

The silence that had pervaded the group before now became an uneasy stir, growing until it erupted in a crescendo of talking and shouting and moving like a riptide through the crowd. Ebb heard the coroner's gavel strike four times before the noise settled to a still uncalm hush.

Ebb swore that the Doc spoke better than any preacher he had ever heard. In the audience, there wasn't an ear that wasn't perked. Doc Cobb stood up again and walked back and forth, pointing toward the audience. His finger passed over Ebb and came to rest at Father DeWitt.

"The ghoul is in every one of us. You. Me. All of us. We hunted down an innocent man, a man we didn't even know—or *care* to know! A man like you and me, who worked in the fields, fished, enjoyed a bottle of beer in the heat of the day. We denied the right to life, the right to struggle to live—even poorly—to a stranger. When the Lord said 'Be merciful to your enemy,' He meant be kind, considerate, and forgiving to everybody . . . Yet, look at us. Which one of us hasn't nursed off the misfortunes of someone else's bad judgment?

"I examined that man's body—the so-called ghoul —and pardon my sayin', but we did him a favor. He didn't die from no gunshot wound. He died a long time before that. If you don't have a good liver . . . if you don't have two good kidneys . . . you don't live too well. If you just have whip cuts and welts for a skin, you don't have much protection, do you? If you don't eat right, if you don't have fruit or vegetables, you're going to have scurvy. His teeth . . ." Doc Cobb pointed

153

to his teeth and made sure everybody looked at them. "All his teeth, his whole mouth, was rotted out. The work of a ghoul isn't easy, you know. Ever try chewin' live chickens? Rabbits? If you're a ghoul and you can't chew, then you don't get fed. Ever try tearin' raw chickens apart with only five rotten teeth and bare gums? Mr. Chickabee Wilson did. He must've been a magnificent ghoul!"

The Doc walked slowly to the side of the room closest to the cloak-room windows. A bee buzzed noisily against the outside screen. Sweat dripped off the old doctor's forehead. The day was heating up fast.

"Twenty-seven degrees nor', nor' west. You all know Moll Legg Island by reputation. Old Black and me went there every time the island had a 'patient.' Only we weren't so fortunate one night in bringing the brethren back. No sir! Like the curse of Job, that body capsized the boat and went floating off in the Patuxent.

Ebb thought of Julius, the tall skeleton that hung in a corner of Doc Cobb's office. He suspected that most of the others in the room were having the same thoughts.

"Yes, I robbed those graves," Doc repeated. As though finally relieved of his guilt, he sat down in the chair and continued. "Forty-two years of grave robbing, bone mending and splinter plucking. That's a long time, isn't it? A long time . . ." He rested his elbow on the arm of the chair and observed his audience with remorse. "Long enough to find out who's who in Calvert County. Long enough to tell what's wrong with most of you without even steppin' through your door. I don't mean that to be derogatory, mind you." The Doc held up his right hand apologetically. "Why, you're the finest folks in the world. There ain't none better. But we, we've got things that ain't so good about us. Things that are wrong. Things that have needed

154

tending to for a long time. We are just a microcosm of the rest of this strange world.

"There hasn't ever been a ghoul! Never! And if there was, then I'm it!! I'm the ghoul. Take a look!" Doc Cobb stood up and pointed to himself several times. "Take a good look! I robbed those graves! I reaped the wealth of flesh that misshaped Moll Legg Island."

Doc hesitated, coughed, and sat down again. He shook his head and continued in a low voice. "Many of you opposed my medical practices, and many, many times I was skeptical in diagnosing one of your ailments. But what I learned from the brethren of Moll Legg, God save their souls, helped me through many an anxious moment. Many a life has been saved. Yet, here I am an accessory to a crime misplaced in time."

Doc Cobb stood in front of Mrs. Bodecker and Jonas. "That wasn't your son who Lare found, Mrs. Bodecker. That was the body of corpse number 13."

CHAPTER 24

"It shook the house and scraped the wall.
He crowed like a rooster and flowed away . . ."

BB straightened up suddenly. The words
of Mrs. Bodecker came to focus on what Doc Cobb had
proclaimed. Without the slightest misgiving, Ebb shot
out of his seat holding his mouth like he was about to
be sick. He had little trouble making his way up the
aisle. The people pushed aside as quickly as they
could. For those who were unaware of the commotion,
Ebb's abrupt appearance hastened their steps aside.
He burst out into the bright sun and stumbled, blinded
by the sudden daylight. He ran toward Talbot's pier.
The boats sat high on the flood, rocking gently on the
tidal swells. A teal-green dory caught Ebb's eye. Without hesitating, he untied the boat and set it adrift along
the jetty toward Boar's pier. He lay on its bottom until
the boat reached the shadows of the wharf. The darkness of the pier relaxed Ebb's apprehension. He listened as the waves lapped against the pilings. When he
was sure that he was out of sight of the schoolhouse,
he set the oarlocks and slipped the green oars into
place. As the boat floated free of the pier, he gave a

mighty heave. The imbalance of the oars, skipping freely over the water, sent Ebb crashing to the back of the skiff. The left oar broke out of his grip and slid into the river. It bobbed in and popped out, easily sliding over the surface and out of Ebb's reach. But he relentlessly pursued the lost oar, and once it was retrieved, his thoughts fastened on Oyster Point and Nelson's Cove.

It wasn't long before the dock faded into the distance. Ebb could barely see the cars lined up on the road. The American flag stood out high and proud in front of the schoolhouse, prompting the thought, "Glad I ain't a nigger."

Rowing to Oyster Point was easier than he had thought. He was indeed amazed that he had come to Nelson's Cove as soon as he had. "Shanty don't scare me none," Ebb said to himself. He beached the skiff and ran straight to Bo's. With due respect, he crowed like a rooster and, out of habit, snuck up to the "honey-house." He went to look in the knothole, as usual, but stopped short on seeing some unfamiliar scratching on the lower corner of the outhouse: "START CIRCUS CLUB EBB-BO."

Tears of joy filled his eyes as he rowed on toward Slough Hen Cove. Ebb noticed that the river had become slack with the changing of the tide. The air had cooled and the crows had started their tidal watch and circled around Brouker's Point. "Jim crabs big, Bo. Gonna be nasty."

Once Ebb rounded Crane Point, he could see Slough Hen Cove in the distance. "Almost a stranger," he thought. Suddenly, he heard a high-pitched mechanical scream in the sky. As he looked up, he saw a navy fighter plane swoop down low over the water. As it passed opposite Half Pone Point, it zoomed upward, releasing a small white parachute which floated slowly

157

to the Patuxent River. Ebb had seen the maneuver all too often and knew the fishing would not be good that day. He held his breath until the explosive sting of the bomb seized the river. In looking southeast, he saw a mountain of water erupt high into the sky.

"Poor fish. They'll die so slow," he thought.

Ebb leaned over the side of the boat and splashed water on his face. The river water was warm and salty. The tide was moving out fast now. He could see the seaweed floating in the shallows.

"Ain't no boy own my body . . . " he reflected.

Schools of menhaden now appeared from the deep, churning the inlet to Slough Hen Cove. Ebb had anticipated stripers or bluefish feeding, but was disillusioned on seeing skate slicing impetuously through the frenzied fish. Just as fast as they appeared, they vanished. The inlet to the cove was once again smooth, revealing the forest of seaweed beneath its turquoise surface. Softbacks and snappers dotted the deep estuary, ducking their heads as Ebb approached.

Ebb's hands had begun to blister, but he stroked steadily until he neared the first sandbar. It was already two hours into the ebb and the water rushed through the mouth of the channel with ominous force. Rather than buck the tide, Ebb let the boat drift with the current until he came to a break in the sandbar, through which he poled quickly into the calm backwash and maneuvered the boat into the shore and up onto the beach. The high, sedimentary cliffs along the entrance to the cove were more foreboding than Ebb had ever remembered—no more the sentinels of boyish fancy. Roots of oak, pine, and elm hung down in entwining masses only to be invaded by the prodigious honeysuckle. Once he had anchored the skiff, he walked back along the beach toward the old fallen oak tree and the magic pool. The tidal pool was still too deep to cross, too swift to swim. Restlessly, he walked back and forth along the shallow shore. The rushing water spilled over the oak's enormous trunk, forming cataracts along its path. From where he stood, he saw the toad marker. The stick was down. There was no sign of life. "Bo's skeleton sittin' in the dark—waitin'," he thought.

Ebb walked up on the bank and sat on the dry sand. He waited and watched, and recalled his uncle saying, "Get past the fog in your mind, son. Don't get mixed in with the poison most people takes."

A half-hour had passed. The channel was now calm at the edge of the far bank. The water tumbled gently over the oak's broken trunk. Seaweed matted each branch with thick, bright-green ribbons, making deep pockets so that each branch hugged a pool of clear, blue water to itself. At its lowest position where the trunk and its branches formed a funnel, the rushing tide flowed fastest and fell to three levels before it mixed back in with the merging river. Ebb and Bo had watched the flow often and knew its signs well.

Ebb looked back across to the hut. "It ain't a proper grave," he reasoned, "but it's where Bo'd wanta be buried." A flash of silver caught his eye and disappeared. He looked back at the magic pool and the falls.

"Ain't you got no mother?"

"Two."

"What's two? You don't got two mothers!"

"You don't know! Just like one that takes care of you is one."

"Dat's not you mother. She's old and . . ."

"Grandma's old . . ."

"Den who's ya other?"

"You a nigger, Bo. I didn't . . ."

Silver again! It sparkled from the river flow. And disappeared. Ebb focused his eyes on the bough of the huge fallen tree. Then he saw it again. A small fish tumbled down the slick, green slide of the oak's branches. Another fish came, then another, until they came slithering down, four to five at a time. They were pogy, slipping and sliding, having themselves the finest time. The pools within the branches were deep—deep enough for the fish to swim in and go out, and swim back for more of the same. But the sand shelf over which they swam was becoming shallow and began to show its crest.

"Three by the toad—three by three. No waitin' now," he assured himself. Ebb crawled onto the oak tree, and moved slowly across its bough. The current buckled forcefully as he moved toward the first branched pool and the white water funnel. Despite his cautiousness, he slipped on the matted slime and tumbled onto the adjacent limbs. The branches snagged him and held him aloft from the current below. Frightened, he moved quickly. With all his energy, he braced himself across the precarious net and lunged for the large branch above the pool. Sensing the branches sinking steadily under his weight, he made one more desperate attempt to free himself. "The calm ain't far," he thought. He forced himself downward to gain upward momentum and, despite the branches giving way to the current, he caught onto the limb and pulled himself to safety. Slowly he moved to the opposite bank.

The toadfish hung as he had seen it before—its mouth agape, its skin hard and greasy. Ebb measured three careful paces from the pole to the middle of the clearing. He stomped his foot three times—three times more. Nothing. Ceremoniously, he stomped his foot again. Again, nothing. His hopes waned to a sadness he had never felt before.

"Bo!" he cried in desperation. "Bo, you there?

160

"Devil, don't get me," he said to himself, and was about to lift up the hatch, when slowly from below the toad pole rose up straight and sure. Ebb stood stock-still and watched the pole go up and down four times.

"Bo, is that you?" Ebb's voice quivered. His body shook with fright and anticipation. He heard nothing. Slowly, he put his ear close to the door.

"Bo, you ain't dead, is ya?

"You hearin' somethin'," Ebb convinced himself. And sure enough, in a distant voice he heard the word "Ebb."

"Bo!" Ebb hollered excitedly. He lifted the hatch quickly. Dirt and sand sifted down through the small opening. He jumped down into the hole and looked into the darkness. In the dim light he saw a silver medallion on a silver chain and a face, "old for what I knowed it." It was Bo.

Candy wrappings were strewn about. Blue and white marshmallow paper and an empty bean can lay in the corner. The musty smell of clay and urine filled his nostrils and burned his eyes.

Bo bowed his head and cried softly. His leg was stretched out in front of him, tied loosely to a rotted board.

"What's wrong, Bo? What'd you do?"

Ebb crawled excitedly over to Bo and sat down by his side. Looking at Bo's leg, he didn't say a word. "Wrigley gum!" he thought. "I've got a piece of Wrigley's gum!" He searched in his pants pocket and pulled out a stick. It was soft and squashed, and hard to unwrap. Ebb gave it to Bo. Bo held the gum indecisively, his thoughts confused by Ebb's unexpected appearance. Slowly, he put the gum to his mouth and commenced to nibble off piece after piece.

"Bo, you hurt?" asked Ebb.

Bo shrugged his shoulders and attempted to move

161

his leg, but at the slightest motion he felt pain and lay back against the dirt wall.

"I'll take care of ya. You wait," said Ebb reassuringly. "Ole Ebb knows all 'bout these things."

It was slow in coming, but the "Bo smile" spread across his face and he finally said, "I . . . I didn't think ya comin'."

"I knowed you'd be here all the time," Ebb insisted.

A white shirt split in fours was wrapped around Bo's leg. "It sure looks good," Ebb said enviously. "I ain't ever had anything like that. How'd you do it?"

Bo stared at Ebb peculiarly, and with great concern unexpectedly asked, "You mind 'bout somebody?"

" 'Bout somebody?"

"You know . . . 'bout da club."

"The club!" The subject struck Ebb as peculiar since Bo was talking about anything but his leg and getting on home.

"Yeah, it bein' all secret and all."

"Yeah."

"If somebody'd say he wanta join the club, and you know he does, and he don't have nowhere to go. He's . . ."

"Bo, if you know somebody's true, that's awright with me. You know that! It's your club, too!"

Bo's spirits rose with Ebb's directness, and he said, "Ebb, you'll like 'em. He's got things to tell ya. Things he done all over. See here!" Bo showed Ebb the silver medallion with the head of a lion.

"When did you tell 'em to come?" Ebb asked.

"He's comin' soon, I know!"

Ebb looked at Bo's leg again. "You feel awright, don't ya?" Suddenly it struck Ebb how long Bo had been gone. "You think he'd mind if we left a note that we's comin' back—'cus ya ma's worried?"

Bo stopped chewing his gum long enough to say,

162

"Well . . . if we writes 'em a good one, he won't mind none."

Ebb began to look around the dim hole for some paper and something to write with. He found some pieces of charred wood and attempted to scratch something on the waxed marshmallow bag. Disappointed, Ebb continued to search until Bo suggested that they use a piece of the shirt wrapped around his leg. Untying one of the sleeves of the shirt, Ebb stretched it across a board and commenced to write, "From Bo." They both leaned back and studied the effect.

Ebb exclaimed proudly, "Ain't that perfect . . ." Ebb congratulated Bo for his ingenuity and put the cloth in a more centered position.

"What you want to say?"

"Tell 'em that . . . that we comin' back soon."

"What's his name?"

"Mista . . . ah, Mista . . . a . . . a . . . um, Chick . . . bee."

Ebb diligently pronounced each syllable as he wrote the name CHICKBEE in big, black letters. When he finished, he looked proudly at his printing, and was about to show it to Bo for approval. Suddenly, Ebb cried out, "MR. CHICKABEE!" and looked over at Bo in disbelief.

"You know Mistah Chickbee!" Bo said assuredly.

Ebb looked at the name again and nodded his head incredulously, and with diligent effort he finished the message. When Bo asked him what he had written, Ebb solemnly read the note: "CHICKBEE—BE BACK IN 1 HOUR. BO AND EBB."

Satisfied, Bo gave a sigh of relief and sat comfortably back against the damp wall. He showed little sign of pain until he tried to move his injured leg. He winced and cursed. Ebb took off his "Sunday shirt" and tied it carefully around Bo's leg. The heat in the hole had

163

gotten intense and made the clubhouse unusually uncomfortable. Bo told Ebb about his visit to the clubhouse and how he had gotten stuck while crossing the tree and the magic pool. "In come the tide. The river woulda tore my leg off if Chickbee hadn't come along. I woulda drown! Chickbee come out of nowhere and saved me." He told Ebb about their staying in the clubhouse and how when Mr. Chickbee saw Bo's suffering, he went to get help.

As Ebb recalled, "I didn't let on for nothin' " and told Bo how brave he was and how they were "goin' get out of this hole." Bo took a big breath and grabbed onto Ebb's back. Bo weighed more than Ebb had expected, but not as much as Honker, he related. Ebb crawled laboriously to the entrance. "You got pride," he thought to himself.

Bo clung to Ebb's neck out of love and need. His skin was rough and thick and dry. Ebb thought of Shanty and Jonas and the blood. He had to spit, and he did. The saliva dribbled down his chin. It annoyingly hung suspended until it slowly stretched to the top of his hand.

The slope of the hole was enough to bring them head-top to the surface. It worried Ebb that Bo's leg might hurt. Beads of sweat popped up on Bo's face. Ebb forced Bo into an upright position and stood him up against the hatch base. This enabled Bo to lean over the side, but because he was so weak, he could not move himself. Ebb quickly jumped out of the hole. Tears welled in his eyes as he watched Bo sustain his pain.

"God, Bo! You gonna make it! Hang on, Bo! You gonna make it! You brave!"

Ebb took Bo's outstretched arms and with all his strength dragged him free of the hole and the smell. The move hurt Bo worse than ever. He screamed like the devil had left his body. But once out in the open, he was calm and lay silently upon the warm, dry sand, looking thankfully to the sky. Ebb gently wiped the sweat from Bo's relieved face.

"You're all right, Bo. Just don't try walkin'. I got the boat right here. You just stay. OK?"

Bo closed his eyes as Ebb took his leave and walked back to the oak tree bridge. The branches were dry. The running tide had subsided and had ceased to flow from the terraced dam. The pools below were shallow, leaving some pogy helpless and glistening in the sun. Ebb shook the branches that held the pockets of fish, but nothing happened. He prodded the captured sand with a stick, and poked the thin, webby seaweed that had meshed together. Small fragments of sand fell from the traps, until suddenly, in one solid mass, the whole pocket collapsed. A whirlpool immediately enveloped the pogy, whisking the fish away to freedom and to their home.

The boat sat high on the beach. Ebb held tightly to the bow and rocked the skiff back and forth across the dry shore until it reached the channel. He tied the moor rope around his waist and pulled the boat into the tidal flow. The swift water ran forcefully between his legs as he tugged against the current, making him lean near head-to-the-water. He pulled slowly and heavy-footed to the magic pool, and to where Bo lay.

It didn't take much persuading to get Bo to the boat. He clung to Ebb, and surprised them both when he found himself sitting high on the bow with little pain or difficulty. Ebb told Bo to hold tightly to the bow while he moved his boarded leg to a safer place. Carefully, Ebb lifted the wounded limb over and into the boat. Bo had closed his eyes in anticipation of the worst kind of hurt. But there was none, and on Ebb's word, he looked down to see his stiff leg resting prone to the gunwale.

165

The sun beamed off his smooth brown face. Ebb could tell he was happy again.

Ebb pulled the boat over the shallow sandbar. Its hull scraped sand and when near to the channel caught tightly to the gravel. He weighed the bow until the boat moved free and steadily. As they entered the channel, he jumped aboard. The swirling current caught the skiff immediately and took it swiftly to the deep.

Gulls and petrel picked on the wet shore. A black man rounded Cove Point perched high on the bow of his skiff, poling slowly along the placid shore, searching for Jimmie crab. "The old crows weren't movin'— just sittin' and carryin' on," Ebb remembered. "It was Bo and me together. I wished it would always be like that."

CHAPTER 25

FOUR YEARS LATER—1952

EOPLE still wake up to the clang of milk cans and to the extravagant crowing of Mr. Goodlittle's rooster. The pace remains slow and thoughtful. The stores are tidy and clean. And Ebb's seat remains well preserved where the old schoolhouse window still faces out over the great river and new eyes and new dreams uphold an endearing tradition of respect and love for the Patuxent. The schoolhouse itself is still painted red and white, and continues to evoke suspicion in those resistant to necessary schooling. However, the old cock weather vane has been fixed. Ebb has long since left eighth grade.

There are some new faces, fewer old faces, and many familiar faces. A bridge now widens the river at Crowells and connects the island with St. Marys County, bringing a weekly caravan of merchants and visitors. In spite of the elders' opposition, the town is experiencing another "boom."

The big circus no longer comes to Prince Frederick. It goes instead to the big cities with their man-made arenas and sterile atmospheres—places to contain peo-

167

ple efficiently while commercial enterprise goes on—predictable and dispassionate. Even the animals seem out of place surrounded by concrete and steel.

Occasionally a small truck-show passes through Prince Frederick, lending an afternoon's excitement and a night filled with music and laughter. The traveling menagerie usually consists of an assortment of small animals, a possum or a raccoon, and, every now and then, a shaggy, ill-fated mountain lion. No Asian elephants. No Bactrian camels.

Recently the good-natured Pastor Eves was seen walking down the middle of town—with a shotgun. He was searching for Fasso. It seems Fasso had rubbed kerosene on the rear end of the pastor's prized bluetick 'coon dog. The poor dog had stayed under Mrs. Damily's house a day and a night, howling away. Everyone thought for sure it was because he'd found himself a 'coon—that is, until they found out otherwise. The feud goes on.

The Chickabee Wilson incident has long passed. As a result of the coroner's inquest the State of Maryland ruled that the death of Chickabee Wilson was accidental. There was no prosecution and Jess Young received nothing but praise for his "outstanding citizenship."

Grievances have been forgotten and a sensible, constructive understanding now prevails in the community. However accommodating, people refer to it as "tolerance." Most of the black people are suspicious of any concerted effort to assuage hard feelings. Many whites carry the guilt of negligence or passivity. There are a few who still live entrenched in their tarnished, misguided tradition, who can neither shake the shroud of prejudice nor displace the veil of discrimination, as there are blacks who will carry the disease of hatred and vengeance to their graves.

There is, nonetheless, a conscious determination to coexist peacefully—however fragile the relationship.

168

Sometimes, however, judging by certain rash, inane incidents, such a peace seemed almost impossible.

It was back in 1950, June 9th. Booker Washington would never forget it, nor would any of the other black people who lived thereabouts. It was the day the song "Nigger Quarter" was coined.

> Quarter for a nigger,
> Hit him on the head.
> Maybe he'll dance a while,
> Even fall dead.
> Hit a nig . . .

Booker knew. He knew the color of the house and the number of ducks that were by the pond that Saturday morning. He remembered the blue shirt and the three pairs of white socks that had been hanging on the clothesline—even the butterfly that floated by. He had been walking home from Durham's grocery store with a loaf of bread under his arm. He whistled and walked briskly. The air was fragrant with honeysuckle. The Duer and the Ring boys were playing marbles on a brown patch of ground where the rope-swing was. He knew each boy only through reference in casual conversation as "the son of Mr. Duer" or as the "boys over at the Rings' place"—never through association. He had been told never to meddle.

As he walked past the yard, a sudden sharp pain exploded in his head. He stopped, momentarily dazed amid a whirl of stars and circles. He shook his head to clear his vision. It was then that he saw all three boys staring coldly in his direction. A strange smile, smug and defiant, crossed their faces as one said to another, "Nice shot!"

Booker looked at the ground. A marble, a bright blue purie, lay at his feet.

"You sonuva bitch!" he cried.

169

The shock of his retaliation stunned the boys. As two of them rose, Booker ran for home. His confidence had been shattered. A code had been broken in a moment of unleashed anger and hatred. Two days passed without incident, but on the third day Mr. Washington came home with rage and fury in his eyes. Sitting down at the kitchen table, he began nervously to tap his fingers.

"What's wrong with you?" Mrs. Washington asked, sensing his uneasiness. And so it was, an uneasiness that uprooted the spirit and brought on despair.

"Do you want some coffee, Jess?"

He didn't answer. He didn't look up. He just stared blankly at the table. His large crusty fingers, dry and caked with the earth, were now folded quietly on the table. He knew what the consequences would be, yet there was a deep sense of pride in his despair. A pride he held for his boy, Booker.

"Booker Washington, a Negro from Solomons, Maryland, called Mayon Duer's son a son-of-a-bitch," read the charge.

"What's this world coming to." The white folk of Solomons, infuriated, hastened to take proper measure. Within a month a court gathering was held. The "insulted" whites filled the courthouse and heard the testimony of the "marble gang" about the loathsome event. The Washington family was condemned for raising such a son as Booker—disrespectful, belligerent.

"Got to keep them in their place, the bastards!"

Each white boy who gave witness merely said "yes" to the question "Did Booker Washington call you a son-of-a-bitch?" and was paid a quarter for his trouble.

And so a precedent was set. Scavenger hunts followed. Whitie sought blackie. "Hit a nigger with a marble. Hit him good and hard. Make him yell and call you names . . ."

"Nobody got rich . . . nor heard a word . . ."

170

CHAPTER 26

significant turning point in Ebb's life was the morning he looked in the old shaving mirror that hung in the outhouse. He had positioned the well-worn "butt" stick in the spot befitting his comfort and sat leisurely thinking of anything other than the chores his grandmother had planned for him that day. He received great satisfaction from looking into the mirror as he abused his good looks by grimacing in a manner usually reserved for "morons." The facial distortions set upon him complimented neither the Kellum family nor any species known to man. The result was always the same. He wondered how God could have made such an ugly creature. This day, however, in the middle of one of his devilish grimaces he saw something that froze his expression. Awkwardly, Ebb traced the contour of his face until he found the spot he saw in the mirror. He marveled at his find. A hair! A real facial hair, however thin and pale, was nonetheless on his chin. The discovery was electrifying. He brushed the follicle tenderly and beamed with pride. After one more look, he burst from the "honey-house" and ran to find anyone who happened to be about—except, of course, for Grandma Kellum. He ran down to Durham's general store where

171

he found, much to his delight, Sheriff Persom, Mr. Henderson and Mr. Durham sitting around the "talking table" sipping their morning coffee.

"G'morning, Ebb."

There was no answer from Ebb, only an air of superiority, a nod of acceptance and an upturned starboard chin. The men looked at Ebb and then at each other with reflective bemusement. Ebb milled about the store with exaggerated aplomb, pretending to be interested in a fly swatter, a tin of chewing tobacco, a fishing bob, an old broken thole pin.

"Hey, Ebb. How's the flat at Nelson's—softies plentiful yet?"

Mr. Durham turned his chair toward the boy as the others looked on. Ebb's chin was so much higher than usual that as he approached the men Sheriff Persom said, "What's wrong with your neck, Ebb?"

"My neck?"

"Yeah, it looks like it pains ya."

And so Ebb's antics through the course of reaching manhood left many with the illusion that he was either struck with the maladies of God's wrath or blessed with abnormal strength and endurance hormones that allowed him to perform remarkable feats of senselessness—acts of bravado—to "prove I can." Only his physical growth bespoke the truth.

It was during his fifteenth year that events took place which proved even bigger than his imagination; that strained, if not almost destroyed, his independent nature. A girl, young and beautiful, came into his life. No one knew how serious the relationship was until the day Ebb and Bo were riding the mule, Eloise, to school. Bo had calmly tolerated Ebb's increasing energies and watched in astonishment as Ebb "grew out of his pants."

Bo's suspicions were confirmed when Ebb plucked

172

off a pine cone and deliberately stuck it under Eloise's
tail. The mule, her ears standing on end, bolted forward toward Jenny's creek with Ebb and Bo hanging
precariously to her mane.

Bo, concerned about Ebb's peculiar manner and convinced that the mule's intention was not to be compro-
mised, accepted the circumstances as calmly as
possible, that is, until they reached the place where
they had intended to stop. As Bo related, "That stop-
pin' place went by like a flash."

"How we gettin' off, Ebb?" Bo asked. There was
much concern in his voice. On hearing no answer, he
looked over his shoulder at Ebb. Ebb, lost in concentra-
tion, was passively urging the mule to an even-faster
gait.

It was on passing Blue Creek Slough that Ebb slid
off the mule's back, leaving Bo and the mule heading
due north at a fast pace reminiscent of Joshua at the
battle of Jericho.

Girls had always held a special place in Ebb's heart,
even if only from a distance, from a safer, more gentle
world than his. His only contacts with girls had been
through an occasional "hello" or some other haphazard
event, most of which were mellow and uneventful.
However, there was one incident, though considered
innocent and expedient by the elders, that left a lasting
impression on Ebb.

"I took a bath with Melanie Todd Richmond! Yes,
sir!" Ebb's face flushed as the soft, sweet recollection
pervaded his memory. And although his words were a
manifestation of his manliness, his hesitant, restrained
thoughts reflected a deep-seated and affectionately
coveted relationship.

I was four years old . . . some time ago. We had
been out at the May Day celebration. All the
townspeople cooked pies and potato salad and

fried chicken and picnicked out along the shoreline of Talbot's farm. In the warming sun they talked about the past winter and the coming summer. Melanie and me picked flowers for the ladies. The fields were full of 'em. Purple and yellow . . . prettiest I ever seen. We was strollin' along and had picked a good lot. Melanie leaned over to pick a buttercup when she points to somethin' and says, "Looka!"

I looked and there was a long black and white stripe movin' along through the tall grass like a snake, mindin' nobody's business but where it was goin'. We didn't know what it was, though the smell was a mite familiar. We followed it. It hesitated. We followed. Suddenly it stopped, got pure mad, left what it was doing and, with its tail stuck straight up in the air, ran right at us—comin' backward! Imagine . . . backwards? It sure was some kinda *skunk!*

You shoulda seen us. We was runnin' and hollerin' and screamin' like we was bein' attacked by goblins. The folks came runnin' up and hollerin' for our lives, but once they found out what had happened, they stopped short and ran back in the opposite direction. There we was, a whole field of people bein' chased by one little ol' skunk. Once we was a safe enough distance away, lookin' back we seen one proud skunk still holding her tail high, stridin' off like she was Cleopatra. And when she come out on the far side of that field, she had seven little babies followin', tail by tail. Cutest things you ever seen. But let me tell ya, that field never smelt the same again. And neither did we.

Melanie and me had to ride together in the back of Talbot's flatbed truck. Nobody else wanted to. When we got to my house, Grandma Kellum had a big, porcelain pan waitin'. It was filled to the brim with tomato juice. In no time at all they had our bathin' suits off and into that pot. Next went me and Melanie! In the same pot! Together! Naked!

I didn't have much time to think about it then. They had us covered with tomato juice, then with soap and vinegar. And Grandma Kellum was scrubbin' with a vengeance. Melanie looked as red as a steamed crab, and as nice and rounded. Even delicious . . . Ha, ha . . . yes, sir. That's what she looked like. When they finally took us out of that pan, I remember how she looked at me with those curious eyes. I . . . always remember those eyes —soft and big . . . curious.

In the recesses of his mind had remained an adoration, an insatiable passion, that would not be smothered by Catholic rhetoric—an ever-present desire fed slowly and continuously by Cupid's whimsical touch. Ebb quickly discarded the cloak of innocence with a fury to pursue his task with enviable yet guileless foresight. Melanie blossomed into her sixteenth year.

"Boy, has she grown! Blue eyes and blond hair . . . long." Ebb saw her occasionally. In his mind she was incomparably beautiful and totally irreproachable. They existed independent of each other until one day the laughter of Miss Melanie Richmond sounded somehow different, no longer girlish or demanding, but mature and mellow. And within Ebb there was an awareness of something natural yet distantly forbidden. This conscious awakening unfolded the mystery and excitement of a whole new dimension—and Melanie Todd Richmond would be ever-present on his mind.

Since the skunk incident, Ebb remembered seeing Melanie many times. But it was not by description that he remembered her; it was by her pet pig, Homer. A piglet of Dorchester descent, Homer followed Melanie to school every day and waited patiently by the school door until dismissal. He would become ecstatic with joy upon seeing her. Jumping up and down on the first wooden step with his short front legs, he would then roll over for a fast scratch on his hard stomach.

Ebb occasionally played with Homer and often marveled at the dedication Homer showed his owner. Enviously, Ebb would slop his own hogs, always accompanying himself with a rash of insults.

"You fat, good-for-nothin, lazy . . ." He would poke them with his pig stick and then shake his head in dismay at their dismal behavior. No matter what his fury or his patience, their character was always simplified by a misplaced grunt or an idle roll in the mud. Usually they stood and looked at him popeyed. Nothing like Homer.

In time, it was an impression of sorrow and grief that psychologically endeared Melanie to Ebb. One windy day in October, he found her weeping softly by a stand of pine trees. Homer sniffed affectionately at her side. But when Ebb approached, the piglet stood curiously defensive. He seemed aware of Ebb's presence, yet didn't appear to see him. In fright Homer sought refuge behind his mistress, only to run headlong into one pine tree after another, until he fell over in bewilderment and dismay. Someone had blinded the piglet with a stick or a gun. (Ebb suspected a BB gun.)

Sympathetically, Ebb laid his hand gently on Melanie's head. He said nothing, just stroked her hair. Then, uncertain at her helplessness and ashamed at his own license, he immediately withdrew his hand and went to retrieve Homer. Ebb walked in front and to her side with protective measure, sad in her sadness, and wondering all the while, "What is a girl?"

CHAPTER 27

THE opportunity to speak to Melanie "seriously" offered itself unexpectedly one April day in front of Talbot's restaurant. She was sitting in the front of her father's car while Dr. Richmond and Ebb's Uncle Elton talked. Ebb and Melanie eyed each other fervently. The "eye-strain" episode might have ended there had not Melanie flashed her eyes with coquettish charm, signaling Ebb to her window.

"Why don't you ask me for an ice-cream soda?"

Ebb, unprepared for this *coup de coeur*, stood dumbfounded. He couldn't utter a word. Melanie turned quickly to the opposite side of the car and peeked out of the window.

"Dad—can I have a soda with Ebb?"

Her father, being unprepared for this sudden request, agreed more in haste than in careful consideration, and looked at Ebb with discerning appraisal. He had never really seen the boy before, that is, not as a suitor to his daughter. Nevertheless, their romance began over a chocolate and a strawberry soda with two glasses of water for Ebb. Three days later they met again for a similar "soda date" and ordered the same thing. This time, however, Ebb didn't have water but he did prolong the sipping of his soda into two and a half hours. As he walked her home, they talked about Jenny Walker's Chinese chicken who had laid green eggs and laughed at the story of the horse with a "buggy" behind. By the third soda date, Ebb ordered the same as Melanie, a strawberry soda, as well as three glasses of water. Having heard that it was not proper to kiss a girl goodnight until the second date, Ebb was convinced that officially this *was* the second date! They both sensed the emotion and stopped short of her house in a shaded knoll to mill about picking off parts of leaves and to talk of trivialities. Finally he cornered Melanie in the outlying branches of a pine tree. With his hands in his pants pockets, he looked to her for assurance.

It was the hardest thing I ever done. Phew . . . was it hard. I said, "Bet you a quarter I can kiss you without touchin' you." I said it so fast, I thought she didn't hear, but she did.

". . . without touching me? Oh—go on . . ." she said.

"Honest. Close your eyes."

"For sure?"

"Yeah."

She closed her eyes and leaned her face close to mine. I leaned over fast and kissed her right on the lips. Her eyes flashed open wide in surprise.

"Why Ebb . . . you said . . ."

I musta looked like cherry-blossom time. "Looks like I lost," I said. "Ain't got a quarter right now, but . . ."

She looked at me, not with suspicion, but with a look I learned meant "Do it again." Everything was singin'. I sure felt good.

After Ebb took Melanie home, he skipped happily up Stripers Lane, his hands still in his pockets, his britches held high. He was proud of the moment and whistled up to the Tilman Creek path, continuing in his long, reflective walk where no one could see his thoughts and where he could be completely alone and secretly in love. Many anxious moments followed before he would see Melanie again. On the next Saturday soda dating became passé. Together they planned a picnic somewhere on a distant beach, shielded from the eyes of Solomons and secluded in their love.

It was a beautiful, sunny afternoon, lively and warm. Puffy cumulus clouds amassed to the southeast while others drifted across the sky billowing and painting the heavens with vignettes—grand and sundry. Some fell from the horizon resembling nebulous veils of woven lace whirling and colliding, and mysteriously dissolving into the magic day. Winter's skin relaxed to the soothing touch of spring's breezes. The big sails of the skipjacks, bellowing and straining to the sea wind, sped their ships steadily toward Cedar Point, across the sound, and beyond. Butterflies danced in the wind and the red-winged blackbirds conversed in their chattering repertoire.

Ebb sat quietly as if in deep contemplation of something distant—out at sea. In fact, the moment was spent thinking, as Melanie too thought, of the agonizing distance between their physical proximity and their physical contact. As he positioned himself on the beach blanket, he accidently touched her leg. He apologized humbly, in a gentlemanly way, and so reserved his most ardent desire—to kiss her for a second time.

Melanie handed him a bottle of Coca-Cola. Their fingers touched. Not for long, and with trepidation. A recurrence—lurid and suggestive. The time had come when there could be no more excuses. Playfully she fed him a potato chip, and then another. A kiss followed. And then another. A cucumber pickle. A third

179

kiss. The fourth kiss, Ebb joyfully said, lasted "forever."

Since kissing was so pleasurable and reserved for those particularly adult occasions, Ebb thought himself worthy of further gentlemanly pleasures, namely, smoking. Thus, Ebb selected his first cigar, an auspicious El Producto Blunt, a fat, stubby cigar. He studied the cigar quizzically and found himself confronted with a task of judgment similar to the case with Melanie Richmond—how to exercise his intent and on which end to exercise it. So he bit what he considered to be the small end of the cigar, tearing far too much of the wad from the stogie. He braved the acid taste of the tobacco leaf and audaciously mouthed the Blunt with pretentious delight.

"It tasted awful," Ebb admitted, "but you shoulda seen Fasso and Jimmy Duer. They looked at me like I was king. I puffed and puffed on it, pulled it in and out of my mouth. I was feelin' bigger and bigger each time I done it, until Jimmy said, 'Ain't you gonna light it?' "

Now a smart remark like that, Ebb had insisted, was uncalled for and as obvious as it may have been, Ebb said that he was going to smoke the cigar. Maybe! However, Fasso quickly lit a match and as Ebb described it, "I went up in a cloud of cigar smoke."

Ebb's eyes watered as he held the smoke in his mouth. He swallowed the smoke slowly, bit by bit, until in one splendid cigar cough, Ebb declared, "I near blew my teeth out."

"Ya all right?" Jimmy asked. Ebb swung around, confused, bug-eyed with disbelief and in a breathless seizure, until Fasso whacked him on his back several times.

"Phew!" Ebb dropped the cigar in the road whereupon Fasso picked it up again. After considering the

180

circumstances, he proceeded to smoke the rancid weed. No one said a word, just watched in amazement as Fasso adjusted to the smoke and began blowing smoke rings with cocky assurance.

Roy Hankerton, the town's banker, drove by and picked them up in his brand-new Hudson. They had driven only a half a mile when Fasso, in sheer desperation and as green as a cucumber, yelled to stop the car. Luckily the door was unlocked, for no more time was allowed for Fasso to find the bottom of his stomach. Likewise followed Ebb. He was as pale as a sheet. As he left the car, he muttered, "See ya . . . aaaa . . . ooooh." Jim Duer looked from the back of the car to see his friends prostrate on the side of the road. Ebb and Fasso lay in the cool, long grass, thankful that they were alive and assured that cigar smokers were indeed a special breed.

Spring passed far too quickly for Ebb. He had seen Melanie every day for the past three months, except for five excruciating days in May when she had visited a distant aunt. Ebb's thoughts were consumed with suspicion. His tortured heart had ached with jealousy. He quickly revived, however, on learning that Melanie had suffered just as much. Ebb, of course, was not about to betray his anxiety. When she did return, he neither called her on the telephone, nor went directly to see her, though painful the wait. But he did stay within hearing distance of the phone. And when the telephone finally did ring, Ebb sprinted from the well to the nearest window by the phone. His heart leapt unmercifully, only to be disappointed. It was Mrs. Damily inquiring about the upcoming fish fry.

"I felt like dying," Ebb admitted. "I lay down on the ground holdin' my chest. I was exhausted from thinking of Melanie Richmond!"

181

The agony of love extended, Ebb fell asleep under the apple tree. Although the sorrel under the shade of a distant willow tree was fanned by a cool breeze, not so Ebb in his shade. He slept in a dream, wet and tormented, drifting helplessly into his Cyprian desires and into the dawning of his manhood:

Two yellow eyes unfolded amid the blackness of a great leopard. The languid animal stared attentively at Ebb from atop a flowery knoll in a vale hidden somewhere deep in the Eden of Ebb's wish, kissed by the sun and replete with a potpourri of brightly colored edelweiss and mountain daisies. In the distance, the mountains caressed the horizon in Florentine pink. The valleys lay lush with bougainvilleas and rhododendron.

The serenity and warmth of this vision moved Ebb deeper and deeper into repose. Suddenly, his mouth fell agape at a vision of Melanie, beautiful as she lay naked in the verdant, soft grasses of a spring. Her silken, blond hair lay fanned about her as she slept. Yet it was not spring, nor any other season Ebb had known.

Deeper and deeper became his trance. Ebb reached out to touch Melanie only to recede and view her instead from afar. Two silver-coated wolves, full-furred and alert, hovered devotedly near her. Patient. Watchful. In a moment of sensation, the forces of Ebb's dream burst forth from their tether. Uncontrolled. Complete.

"Ebb . . . Ebb! It's Melanie!"

CHAPTER 28

EBB sat in deep thought at his desk. The upper bounds of the desk contained three shelves, the lowest of which displayed an assortment of paraphernalia set there for reference, adornment or out of fondness. His stare was clouded in a moment of dreaminess, neither here nor there, until the realization dawned on him that where there had been two bucktail lures and a white-feathered jig, there were now only the two bucktails, one yellow with green eyes and the other white, skirted with red eyes "like rubies." He absentmindedly brushed the button of the white lure with his fingers and thought of the third, missing lure and of a fish, the story of which he would tell over and over again in his repertoire of fish stories—the fish that got away—"that fish."

It had been a day in early April, one year and a half earlier. The weather was intermittently rainy. There was no wind and once the drizzle had stopped, the river became smooth and reflected depths of blackness.

Ebb had borrowed his Uncle Elton's boat with its small five-horsepower Johnson outboard engine. The old motor puttered along as Ebb held the throttle to trolling speed and moved slowly across the rocky bot-

tom off Helen's Bar. The drone of the motor would have
been lonely had it not been for the expectation of fish.
Ebb was alert and held tightly to his trolling rod as his
white lure kicked along the bottom. There were no
signs of fish feeding, yet Ebb sensed an event in the
deep calm, a movement of some kind, an awareness. It
was on his second pass that his rod bent viciously from
the thrust of a hooked fish—an eleven pound striper.
After nine turns, Ebb had boated twelve fish, the biggest being seventeen pounds. It was on the twelfth pass
that Ebb thought he had hooked onto the bottom of the
river. The rod snapped forward with unmitigated force,
bearing on to break the pole as the drag gave naught.
Ebb quickly released the pressure from the reel and
the fishing line spun out in a fury toward the drift and
the middle of the river. He tightened the drag again
when there was a sudden great rush as the line sliced
out over the water and rose as it strained to the weight.

There Ebb vaguely saw the black and white stripes
of a huge bass as the fish continued on its journey. The
line went slack and so was lost a great fish and a number seven white-feathered jig.

"That fish" was "Old Greenhead," who now moved
in the solemn wake of a large school of striped bass
many miles to the north-northeast. The healing scar
caused by a large hook told its story as did all the other
scars this anadromous fish bore. As Ebb dreamed on,
Greenhead made ready to revisit the Patuxent and his
home in the sweet water.

It was a pleasant, clear ocean day. The surface water
was calm and serene, reflecting the great orb of October's new moon. Even Old Greenhead could see
fathoms beyond his accustomed view in these recent
summer waters. The Gulf current now infused the rich
Grand Banks and the Arctic currents with an abun-

184

dance of newly oxidized waters. As the winter solstice approached and took its course, the shelves of summer plankton sank to the bottom feeders.

The lethargic schools of striped bass milled uneasily off Georges Bank, the seasonal migratory urge awakening in their bodies. The mature females were plump with eggs and snapped agitatedly at the big males as they nudged them playfully. But as the constellation Cepheus became higher in the sky, the casual prod became more frequent, more demanding until, en masse, the huge, meandering school charged with turbulent energy in solid exodus toward its distant breeding ground. For all it would be heroic. For many it would be final. And for an enduring few, it would mean old life renewed.

Old Greenhead was a magnificent fish of some 130-odd pounds. At 48 years old, he had lived long past his prime, but he continued to join the others in the yearly migration up the great estuary of the Chesapeake Bay, into the warmer, brackish waters of the Patuxent River, onward to the fresh feeder streams of its many tributaries, on to where the beginning of new life unfolded in splendid ritual. He had tired of the rock fights and often sought the solitude of the rocky shore off Rhode Island and Massachusetts, but this year the scent of the pilgrimage was strong to him, stronger than ever before. He was glad. The shelf was now the home of many old, unproductive fish—fish who followed the ritual only to return to the great ocean, which was now more barren and depleted of life's chain.

Even the sounds were foreboding and distantly forlorn. The echoes of life were no longer plentiful as in years past. No longer did the great sperm whales glide through the lavish plankton fields along the great coastal estuaries, with their distended jaws filtering the vast ocean harvest in silent pleasure. The bottom

185

dwellers were disappearing and the pelagic roamers of the surf swam in confused patterns of uncertainty. They could no longer smell their source. Already some were the victims of change, larger and older than their predecessors. Some were infertile and almost hermaphroditic; many were part of a dying species.

Despite the signs of danger, they swam on toward Hudson Canyon. Where movement and contrast had once been their world, now only a desert existed, opaque and lifeless. The sea meadow now lay bare where once there had been a constant motion of silver and green and shimmering blue. The hydroids were gone. No more moss animals; the prawns and crabs had moved south. The school of stripers swam in a search pattern, meandering slowly, unsure. The temperature of the waters was mixed, too mixed to navigate with certainty. The great herd created wave lengths which fell dead in the lifeless basin of the New York Bight. No light filtered its depths. No food. Only sludge and industrial waste washed in its waters. Where clouds of river herring and shad had once gathered at the vortex of the great North Atlantic drift, now only giant oil slicks slid aimlessly through the once rich egg beds of the dying shoal, contaminating the life-giving plankton. No longer could the fish of the Hudson smell the waters of their birth.

Suddenly, there was a noise. In fright, Greenhead swam quickly to the right of the school. He had heard the sound before, but listened intently to be sure. It was a voice, real and deadly. He swung quickly back to the front of the column to split the herd for retreat in either direction. But the maneuver was too late. As the first band vaulted to the left, its front line disappeared in a cloud of crimson, cleaved in a whisper as the mountainous bulk, the Great White Shark, plowed its course. Confused, the right flank of the school swam back through the carnage and retreated to the north.

186

Greenhead looked back upon the suspended death. There he saw young Squidhound, a six-seasoned striper, swimming in helpless circles, a milky substance oozing from his sleek white underside. The wound was visceral. As Greenhead swam away, the lactescent fluid waxed redder until the stream of blood issued scarlet, then blended with the sea, turning black against the cold light. The awesome killer once again appeared, this time to the smell of blood. Its shadow rose ominously from the depths, its great jaws menacingly drawn for the kill, repulsive, sadistic. Unmindful of its perfect measure or its destructive force, the shark struck Squidhound violently, carrying the big fish forward with effortless speed. The striper's flank shivered on impact; the fish was gone, his hysterical, agonizing, repetitious bleating lost in the frenzy of fleeing fish. Only his head remained, his eyes neither alive nor dead, expressionless. It was the last of Squidhound as his remnants slowly sank to the bottom.

Greenhead sped quickly into the muted depths. There were no wasted motions now, no meandering. They must escape. Only when the sterile plains below grew fertile and rose high on the Continental Shelf and the Baltimore Canyon did the school relax and take account of its position. The strong rush of the autumn currents still brought no scent of their breeding place. However, Greenhead did feel the vibration of a small school of mullet passing along the distant bank. Moving closer to its source his excitement intensified, for there, just ahead, was what he loved best, the white rough waters of the New Jersey coast. His broad tail flipped joyously as he left the herd and joined in the gusto of the pounding surf. A great northwest wind licked the sea, blowing the surface waters outward and upward. Giant waves crashed tumultuously, plowing the depths in relentless, sweeping runs, swirling and mixing its waters with the life-giving elements. Greenhead rolled and raced in their crests, his iron-gray back slicing the breaks as they curled in the sunlight. So, too, the mullet played in the surf, but this time their fate was sealed. Greenhead, immersed in the ecstatic frenzy of the moment, gorged himself. Other stripers soon joined the feast. The water now rippled in a fury of mindless greed. The wind and the sea gulls danced above the silvery swarm. The rock fed long and then, suddenly, disappeared toward the Chesapeake estuary.

One fateful night soon after, a strong southeast wind blew the sea high into the estuary. With the moon full, it moved the tides deep into the inlands. Once the drift had spilled its banks with exceptional rout, the waters raced from the streams and the rivers into the bay and onward to the ocean where schools of fish—stripers, shad, croakers, and drum—waited with heads to the current. Greenhead listened and smelled. There was no mistake. This was the source—the time. But something was wrong. Something toxic and acid was in the water. The school lingered momentarily, then hesitantly swam forward. They passed other meandering schools of fish whose time would come. But the increased salinity of the estuary made it difficult for the stripers to excrete the salt from their own bodies.

Suddenly the water exploded before them. The school scurried to the right and to the left. Frightened, Greenhead watched attentively until a small break in the churning water revealed a black wall of marauding eels. They slithered easily back and forth across the channel, striking the full-bodied females at random, tearing their soft underbellies and mouthing their eggs with malign relish. But still, something more was wrong. Greenhead drank heavily where he seldom drank. Alarmed, he turned back toward the ocean. Many females were now floating disemboweled, fodder to the sea. Other females and males sank helplessly—

dehydrated. The school swam on, farther into the ocean. Ten, twenty-five, fifty miles. Never had they gone so far. Here, among the steep palisades, the silent mackerel slept in winter. Still disturbed, Greenhead and his school swam past the escarpments to where the salinity became bearable—onward into the deep blue depths, into the darkness to await another day, another journey to the beckoning call of the Chesapeake Bay and the Patuxent tributory.

EVER was Ebb so miserable or his thoughts more radical as on that balmy August night in 1952. Ebb and Melanie had met, much to Ebb's consternation, on the Richmonds' porch. There, supervised by Dr. and Mrs. Richmond from the distance of the nearest window, the two young lovers sat on the porch swing talking and sneaking kisses in the early night. Then the window light went out and Mrs. Richmond authoritatively knocked on the adjoining wall, signaling her daughter to speed Ebb on his way and to come to bed herself. At this juncture in their romance, emotion was at its highest pinnacle; to leave meant forever, and tomorrow, never.

It was on occasions such as these that Ebb's imagination was stimulated toward a young man's fancy. This evening, his inclination was particularly strong. With the courage of Marlborough, he proposed a tête-à-tête, a meeting that night—secret and forbidden.

The night was mellow as the countryside slept content in the warmth of a summer's breeze. From atop a towering pine in back of Ebb's house a nightingale sang. The intrusion of a leg, two arms, and finally the emergence of a whole body sent it flying. It was Ebb sneaking out of his bedroom window onto the roof.

190

Carefully, he replaced the window screen, stole quietly to the "possum" tree, and wound slowly down the old, twisted wisteria shrub that adorned its bough. A bright light was shining through the living-room window. Ebb, hanging by his legs from the appropriate branch, watched his grandmother furtively. The joys of this intrigue welled in his body as he dropped deftly to the ground, ran to the well, and scurried onward to his rendezvous.

In the bright light of the moon the beach sparkled as the river meandered along its shore. Spike rushes and pickerel weeds punctuated the shallows where aurelia danced. Sandpipers ran to and fro. Herring gulls, surprised at the intrusion into their solitude, screeched angrily and flew up in annoyed confusion as Ebb passed through their sanctum. The magic of the night was everywhere. Even the ghost crabs, unseen, exuded an essence of nocturnal bliss as they scurried blithely over the Patuxent sands. Ebb crossed Tilbet's Shoal and climbed up onto the far bank. Following its winding path to the Richmonds' meadow, he pressed onward to their house. Tall trees stood out distinctly in the moon's projected light, covering the ground in a wash of silvery glaze. As he approached, an Irish setter rushed from the shadows and barked twice, but upon recognizing Ebb wagged its tail in greeting and followed happily at his side. Silently hugging the contour of the house, Ebb came upon Melanie's bedroom window. He threw a small pebble which sounded a thump in the night and was followed by a chorus of crickets. He picked up another stone and was about to throw it when he stopped short. There, in the window frame, rose a head, the outlines of which seemed akin to Medusa! Ebb stood dumbfounded. Slowly the shimmering waves of lunar refraction molded the illusion into the vision of a lovely young girl.

191

Melanie smiled. In the quiet of her room she slipped from sight, and with a conviction born of independence, however right or wrong, however fateful, followed the stirring desire of her youth. They met beyond the hedgerow on the gravel dirt road and walked on into the night, barefoot and fancy-free.

"Aren't you scared?" Melanie tripped along by Ebb's side, absorbed in his persistent, omniscient charm.

Ebb, thinking the question girlishly naive, retorted with manly indignation, "Heck—what's there to be scared of?" Then, he commenced to relate a string of the most unruly stories. Ebb's improvisation and exaggeration would have made Satan bite his tongue. With great pride he showed her the scar on his back, the cause of which, Ebb explained, was "fightin' oyster thieves and float snatchers." Melanie stared at the scar in admiration, thrilling Ebb and inciting further swagger.

"Nothin's gonna hurt you. . . ." Firmly he took her hand in his and together they walked toward Cromwell's watermelon patch.

The melon field was set back thirty yards from Rock Road, concealed by a honeysuckle fence and tall grass. Ebb had a touch for watermelon and it was to his sheer delight that he tapped the first melon and heard the hollow thump of ripeness.

"Yeah, they're ripe." So saying, he broke the vine and handed the melon to Melanie.

"Go on," he whispered. Excitedly, she ran toward the road, only to trip over a small hedgerow and land on top of the melon. The large fruit broke into three pieces, but there was no time for regret, for the noise, though subtle, had alerted the Cromwell dog. Ebb ran awkwardly onto the road, his arms bowed with two large melons, the weight of which impaired his gait. He and Melanie disappeared into the darkness and together ran gleefully toward Talbot's swimming hole.

They arrived breathless and arm weary and lay on the dry, warm sand to rest and feel the mellowness of the summer night's air. After the anxiety of haste had settled, Ebb and Melanie sat up to observe their spoils, wondering what they were going to do with two large watermelons, especially since they had no knife with which to cut them. They considered the situation until Ebb, in a fit of indecision, playfully kicked one of the melons, sending it barreling down the sandy hill into the river. In his retrieve, he thought to split the fruit on Talbot's diving board, and so he did, losing half of the melon as it slipped from his anxious hands. But the other half was held tightly and coveted as he carried the prize to Melanie's side—theirs to enjoy and eat with relish. Watermelon juice dribbled from their chins onto their hands and their arms and wet their clothes. The air smelled sweet with its flavor. The mosquitoes stayed aloft in the soft southeast breeze, as did the indulgent fireflies.

Ebb, in his sticky, uncomfortable state, decided to go swimming. He stood up on the diving board and searched the enclosure to see if any sea nettles had gotten past the retaining net. Convinced there were none, he motioned to Melanie to join him whereupon they both stood together on the platform and jumped off the diving board in one fine "suicide" leap. The water was warm and briny. They swam in wide leisurely circles, each lost in thought, wishing this night never to end. They emerged refreshed and sat on the beach. Ebb remained silent for a long moment slowly piecing his thoughts together until the discomfort of wet clothes confused his emotions. Melanie's hand searched for his and, finding it, prompted him to move closer to her. He rolled on his side and followed her movement as she lay back not hesitantly now, but with confidence and closeness, more familiar and relaxed in their love. He nuzzled her gently.

"Kinda uncomfortable, ain't it?" Ebb sat, little realizing that his movement had pre-empted a more sensitive gesture from Melanie. The rejection, however slight, led Melanie to suspect the night's magic soon would end. She did not notice the serious reflection in Ebb's eyes as he adjusted his position. The mixture of seawater and sand shriveled his skin and itched "somethin' awful."

But the magic of that night did not end. Regardless of his exasperation from physical discomfort, the events that followed were by chance beautiful and untainted.

Ebb sprang suddenly to his feet and ran to the diving board where he dove into the soothing, deep dark pool once again. The water engulfed him in its silence as he swam steadily downward. Only when his air was nearly exhausted did he release his grip on the river to float serenely to the surface and slowly swim toward the river bank. When his hands touched the narrow shoal he looked up and saw Melanie.

"It's more comfortable in here." Ebb gestured, and floated quietly in the stilled night now confident that her eyes followed his every move.

Melanie dipped her toes in the water and gently slid down the steep, sandy bank of the river channel. She submerged quickly beside Ebb and bobbed back by his side. Killifish darted here and there as the two youths frolicked and kicked about on the shallow bank. The foreboding cry of a loon drifted in the warm, moonlit night as Ebb softly kissed Melanie. But the kiss lasted and lasted until Melanie, in her anxiety, pushed Ebb away.

What Ebb had assumed to be a freedom was now measured with timid restraint. At first, he confused fright with desire as she backed away.

"Somethin' wrong?" Ebb looked about the water as

if he assumed a nettle or a crab had bitten her. But there was a silence of uncertainty as their eyes met, something foreign in her gaze rendering Ebb helpless and naive to their difference.

Hesitantly, Melanie said, "We're kissing . . . li . . . like . . . we're married."

Astonished, Ebb looked down at the water with perplexed emotion. "What's wrong with that?"

"Father Mullen says kissin's all right, but married kissin' . . . it's different."

"Married kissin'!!! Married kissin'!!!" Disillusioned by the thought of what might mean no more kissing like "real kissin' " or what Father Mullen called "married kissin'," indeed Ebb was disturbed.

"You tell 'em . . . 'bout kissin' and all that?"

Shyly Melanie admitted that she did "sometimes." The word perceptibly renewed his energies—"married kissin' " or "no kissin'." With a twinkle in his eyes, Ebb said, "Well, let's try kissin' with . . . without bein' like married . . . what's he say 'bout huggin'?"

In his sex, Ebb suddenly felt sure. He assured Melanie that they indeed "shouldn't kiss like married folk or anything like that." Thus they settled in the comfort of their embrace and rationalized the art of kissing, assured that they did no wrong even if their hearts pounded unmercifully. They lay together in the sleek softness of the risen moon, content and in love as two Parrish youths. Again the loon called into the night. The eddies spun out toward the open sea as the ebb took force and pointed the channel markers southeast. This night's kiss would be told to Father Mullen and forgiven with three "Our Fathers" and six "Hail Marys."

CHAPTER 30

EBB awoke the next morning feeling strange. Although the sun was shining, he felt as if he had awakened in an eclipse—silvery and dark, shiny and eerie. No reason, he thought. A warm breeze blew in with the morning light. It was peaceful. But the cock's crow was hollow, even sad. Ebb jumped from bed and looked outside. There was nothing unusual to catch his eye. Faintly he could hear the distant rustle of the shimmering wheat. Quickly, he pulled on his pants and left the house by the front door. He walked cautiously to the oak tree. Puzzled, he looked out over the Patuxent River. Something was wrong. The river lay in a deep hush, deeper than before a storm. An uncertain feeling began to taunt Ebb as his eyes slowly scanned the horizon. His emptiness grew as the voice of silence spoke ever truer. Finally he accepted the inevitable message that his heart and soul had felt. Poe was dead.

Ebb didn't go to see Poe, he just watched from the distant corn field as four of the townsfolk carried his body from the old house in a pine-board coffin. Ebb cried softly and thanked Poe for being his dearest friend.

A year later, he did visit Poe's abode. The place had not changed. Weeds and vines had always adorned the premises, except that now the berry and rose bushes were full of fruit and flowers and the grasses were knee high. No more a banquet to the persistent Nubian goats that fed pellmell thereabouts.

Poe's Model T Ford sat stoically in the vine-covered garage, its original tires still like new. Ebb cranked the old water pump. It squeaked mercilessly and smelled of lime. On the third pump a small green snake slithered, frightened, from its funnel and scurried anxiously through the weeds. The incident provoked the memory of a buzzard Ebb had accidently shot some years ago. In attempting to help the wounded bird, he was held off by its outstretched wings. The bird, tired and exasperated, lowered its ugly head and floundered backward in spasms of regurgitation—its fresh meal of a young cottontail rabbit lay before him as if the bird wished to give back what it had eaten in exchange for its freedom.

Ebb mounted the back porch stairs and opened the squeaky screen door. It had always squeaked on opening and always banged shut when it closed.

"Dang thing. Gotta fix that dang thing," Poe would tell Ebb. Ebb said that Poe would grab the door and give it a couple of shakes, then close the door softly, saying it was "OK."

As he entered the kitchen, there was an emptiness which was both sad and forlorn. Ebb walked directly on to the bedroom. He stopped in the hallway as he saw the skeleton of an animal near Poe's bed. The bones did not complain, but lay in resignation and devotion. They were the bones of Mary, Poe's favorite Nubian goat. He had nurtured her at birth, the nanny goat having died from pneumonia. Poe had bottle-fed her with the milk from another goat. He had loved her

197

dearly and watched over her constantly; they even ate and slept in the same room together. Ebb's Uncle Elton had told him that they had found Mary standing by Poe's bed when they arrived to remove Poe's body. They could neither budge the goat, nor coax her to leave the room. She did not eat or drink. Finally they left her, but she never left Poe's bedside.

Ebb said good-bye to Poe's house for the last time, shook the squeaky old screen door and started across the unplanted field. As Ebb turned his head for one last look at Poe's house, he heard a "swoochooooo . . ." Turning back, he saw the fleeting image of a bird gracefully sweep up to the heavens, into the blinding sun, and then disappear. What had it been? Never before had he heard the sound, this small projectile rending the air and controlling the environment with smooth, unfaltering precision. "No osprey. Too small. No kingfisher. Not a sparrow hawk." Ebb waited and searched the sky, but saw nothing and continued to walk. Seconds passed when he heard screeching, a derisive burst of energetic gibber. Looking up, he saw a hawk he'd never seen before, a peregrine. To his amazement the falcon rolled in the air and then suddenly swooped as if to kill, dropping swiftly out of sight. The victim of his sortie, a large buzzard, flew upward in disgust and was antagonized in his lumbering flight by the effortless aerobatics of this playful adversary. Occasionally the hawk would roll on his back and in mid-air, with talons outstretched, clip the buzzard's breast, striking lightly enough to loosen a claw of feathers; not to kill but to vex. To test and refine his ability. To stay alert and to enjoy. Tomorrow he would hunt.

Ebb pondered the subject, how nature carried on, how life was so wonderful in so many ways—in so many things. Things that could not be explained. Important things. Things that were just of God and himself. He thought affectionately of Melanie—her desire for children and her need for love—the moments spent together in joy and understanding. Her closeness. It was only yesterday, he thought, that she had brought a drink of lemonade to him in the field. He had been helping Mr. Cromwell load hay. Mr. Cromwell's little girl, in the excitement of the day, skipped joyfully over the moist morning clover. On hearing the gleeful response, even the cows looked up from their grazing to see the occasion. Cupped in her hand she gingerly held something close to her bosom. Ebb had stopped his chore and watched the lass as she ran skitily-skut up to her father. Absorbed in her find, the girl didn't look up, but held her hand close to her left eye with the intensity of a microbiologist looking through a microscope. A skewed-up lower lip and a hard-pressed left eye gave the impression of intense deliberation. Once satisfied with her elusive quarry, she held this remarkable discovery carefully—very carefully—up for her dad to see. Slowly, nervously, she separated her reluctant palms, when suddenly into the daylight jumped one exasperated bullfrog. The girl's eyes popped in disbelief as the amphibian plopped to the ground. Whether surprised or stunned by his sudden release, the frog sat with closed eyes, mesmerized in the warming sun. Both the girl and the father got to their knees and studied the amphibian with respectful, concerned appreciation and wonder.

Ebb smiled and walked on to the river's edge and along the shore. He thought of what Poe used to say about the watermen of years ago, about knowing how "they got somethin' " and "the best thing was, they knowed the next day was gonna be somethin' of the same." Ebb knew he had "somethin'." For this he was grateful. But now as he looked out over the calm Patux-

199

ent, he deeply wondered about "the best thing" and instinctively feared for the next day, not for himself but for those to follow. Would there be something of the same?

EPILOGUE

Lo, the anxious wings of night that beat this stormy
dawn.
These birds of Lazarus, blindly searching,
Whistling, calling wildly in day's tempestuous wake.
Hark, you boreal wind, cold and poised on trembling
haunches;
Who stalks this earthen creature without pity.
A brazen sun dares lift its fiery head above the river's
plain.
Through driving snow and blizzard's path, a guiding
light I see.

Chase Ezekiel Kellum

Glossary

Chapter 1

Big Jim—Name used by Eastern shore people for the male blue-shell crab—also Jimmie.

Pogy—Another name for the fish menhaden.

Fish hawk—Osprey.

Bugeyes;

Skipjacks—Names given to sailing vessels.

Tong—To dredge oysters.

Patrol—Oyster patrol.

Hardhead—Name for a fish—croaker family.

Chum—Bait fish.

Chapter 2

"Water could be drunk"—Refers to the salt content in the river; 25 to 30 parts salt per thousand parts of water required for female crabs (known as sooks) to spawn the following spring.

Chapter 4

Black bricks—Bricks treated by heating them red-hot and dipping the exposed surface into melted coal tar.

Clean bucket—Unmuddied water.

Chapter 5

Buster—A crab in that period of growth when its shell is between hard and soft.

Spot;
Hardhead—Fish—members of the croaker family.

Chapter 7
Bushtail—Squirrel.

Chapter 8
Canvasbacks—Canvasback ducks.
Divers—Diver ducks.
Hunting blind—A place of concealment while hunting.

Chapter 10
Channel bass—Member of the croaker family. Another name for the drumfish.

Chapter 11
Trot line—Fish line arranged with several hooks for attaching bait or bait tied at intervals. Used to attract hard crabs.
Patuxent ribbons—Varied shades of blue which appear on the Patuxent River in the spring.

Chapter 12
Busters;
Shedders;
Soft/Hard—Names for crabs during different phases of their growth.
Doubler—Male and female crab together.

Chapter 14
Anadromous fish—Fish which ascend rivers from the sea at certain seasons for breeding.

Chapter 18
One-armed bandits—Slot machines.
Drum—Drumfish is a member of the croaker family—August run.

Chapter 19
Pumpkin ball—Shotgun shells used to hunt big game.

Chapter 24
Skate—Salt water food fish of the ray family; winged bodies.

Chapter 26
Thole pin—A wooden or metal pin set in the gunwale of a boat to serve as a fixed rest against which the oar presses in rowing.

Chapter 28
Troll—To trail a bait astern.
Bucktail—An artificial lure with wings of fur or hair.
Jig—A lure used in trolling that has a blunt, bullet-shaped metal head to which is bound a mop-like tail of feathers.
Brackish waters—Water that is not fresh or running; saltish, hence stagnant and ill-tasting.
Rock fights—Striped bass fighting for dominance.
Pelagic roamers—Fish which roam the open sea or ocean.
Rock—Another name for striped bass.

Chapter 29
Killifish—Bait minnows.

ABOUT THE AUTHOR

RICHARD C. MEARS was born in Baltimore, Maryland, in 1935. Descended from a line of sea captains and plantation owners, he was well schooled in Southern tradition. Tragedy in his early life sent him into seclusion where he sought refuge on the Chesapeake estuaries and particularly on the Patuxent River. Here he acquired a deep knowledge and love of the river, its wildlife and woodlands. Sensing his pending academic doom, his father sent him to a private boys' school taught by the Jesuits in the classic tradition. Lacking the financial means to attend a university, he enlisted in the U.S.A.F. to qualify for the G.I. Bill. After three years of intelligence work, world travel and study, he entered Pennsylvania State University and graduated in 1961 from the School of Journalism. He tested careers in New York City in T.V. film production, agency advertising and investment markets. He now is president of his own investment corporation and spends his time with his artist wife and their children between their historical inn in the Berkshires in Massachusetts and their home in Northern California. *Ebb of the River* is his first novel.